CW00500270

*Also by Steven Key Meyers*

### Fiction

*That's My Story*
*Save the Max Man!*
*A Family Romance*
*My Mad Russian*
*The Wedding on Big Bone Hill*
*Springtime in Siena*
*Queer's Progress*
*Good People*

### Non-Fiction

*The Man in the Balloon:*
*Harvey Joiner's Wondrous 1877*

### Plays

*A Journal of the Plague Year,*
*and Other Plays and Adaptations*

# *All That Money*

A Novel

Steven Key Meyers

*All That Money*

Copyright © 2021 Steven Key Meyers

Published by Steven Key Meyers/The Smash-and-Grab Press

ISBN 978-1-7368333-0-8

All rights reserved. No part of this publication may be reproduced, stored in a retrieval system or transmitted in any form or by any means — electronic, mechanical, recording or otherwise — without the prior written permission of the author.

All characters appearing in this work are fictitious, except for historical characters treated fictionally. Any resemblance to real persons, living or dead, is coincidental.

A 2011 edition of this book was published by BookLocker.

Revised Edition 2021

**SMASH**
&GRAB
**press**

*All That Money*

*For my father,*
*who helped make this a better book*

"So there you are. The prospect of all that money completely devastated my morals."

Dashiell Hammett
*$106,000 Blood Money*


"Them rich dames are easier to make than paper dolls."

Raymond Chandler
*Farewell, My Lovely*

# I.   March 1934

## 1.

FALLS CITY—*Falsity* in the charming local drawl—sprawled beneath the Spode Tower, at 14 stories high the tallest structure (excepting steeples) between Cincinnati and St. Louis. Its height gave upper-floor occupants sweeping views of the city lying along the broad silver slash of the Qwattata River. The unhurried wash of the river above and below the city set the Southern tempo that Falls City luxuriated in, though for half a mile rushing past downtown it was a boiling rapids.

But in his office in the tower's crown, Robert Spode, Jr. saw only the letter lying on his desk.

He read it again:

March 7, 1934

Dear Bob,

It is with confidence in your generous character that I write to beg a favor.

You will remember when we raised
your fine Tower several years ago
that my son Harry was proving a
trial to me. He has since left
Vanderbilt Law School under a cloud.
He is at heart a good young fellow,
so quick in his parts that I retain
my fondest hopes for his future.

But given the dismal business
climate here in Memphis, not to
mention the propinquity of the young
lady in question, might I ask your
help in finding Harry a job in Falls
City? Whatever be the work, however
humble, I promise he will perform
his duties well. Occupation and a
change of scene will help my boy
grow up.

Please, Bob, make everlastingly
grateful

Your humble servant,
Vergil Thrall

Pressing a button, Spode spoke into an intercom: "Miss Bryant, please take a letter."

Miss Bryant came in and sat down, demurely crossing her legs. Getting to his feet, Spode frowned outdoors as he dictated.

"Dear Vergil, It is a pleasure to hear from you, although a pleasure shadowed by your son's—*um*—vicissitudes. As a father I sympathize. Fortunately my daughter Lucie since her marriage has ceased giving me cause for worry. I recommend marriage for your son.

"Paragraph. Although I wish I could help, given present

business conditions—"

Miss Bryant cleared her throat. Looking at her, Spode remarked, "Thrall's a good man. Wish we had a place for this cub of his, but distillery's only place we've hired since the Crash, and it's full up."

"Things are so slow, Mr. Spode," Miss Bryant said. "But I did hear that Charlie at the Spiral Garage found his day man siphoning gasoline and let him go."

"*Oh!* That might do," said Spode, nodding. "All right: By all means, send Harry to me, should he be willing to work as— What do we call it, Beth?"

She blushed at the working-hours lapse of formality.

"Parking attendant?"

"—parking attendant at the Spiral Garage. Compensation is slight—$2 a day, plus tips, and as you might imagine, tips have fallen off since Wall Street brought these hard times upon us. Still, your son should be able to keep body and soul together.

"Paragraph. The Spode Tower continues to answer every purpose we had in mind for it, although had we foreseen the current business depression a smaller structure might have sufficed.

"I remain *et cetera, et cetera.* Type that up right away, please."

Wreathed in the glow of benevolence, Spode admired his city of limestone, gazing past the pennants snapping above the Spiral Garage to where the breeze lifted plumes from the tailings overhanging the Spode cement mills and Spode quarries. Sunlight glanced off the water towers and warehouses of the Spode distillery, while the neighboring Spode pipe foundry belched gray; before the Depression, when it operated at capacity, the foundry's inky smoke obscured the whole valley.

Nearer, a spider web of iron bridged the river with train

tracks; the Falls City & Atlanta Railroad was not solely a Spode enterprise, but the family held large minority positions in it.

Away off to the west, Spode traced the fine neighborhoods stretching along the Qwattata, especially the bluffs surmounted by Indianola Farm, the old Spode slave plantation where he and his father still lived. The roof upheld by white columns was all that could be seen of the mansion, next door to the patterned brick chimneys of Overridge, where his daughter lived with her husband. A spyglass might have disclosed his ancient parent in his Bath chair, at 97 his Civil War regiment's sole survivor, soaking up sun beside the boxwood hedges, leaning against his nurse like a suckling babe against its mother.

Miss Bryant carried in his letter and he signed it.

However satisfying the view, there was work to be done.

## 2.

THE FOLLOWING MONDAY morning when the elevator operator heaved open the brass doors to his aerie, Spode saw Miss Bryant giggling.

At the wall opposite her slouched a young man in a dark, close-fitting suit. Merely by adjusting his cuff — but doing so with a dazzling smile — he raised a blush on her face that, as her boss entered, she tried to finesse by reaching a hand to her bun.

Spode strode into his office. Miss Bryant followed and helped divest him of hat and coat.

"Who's that boy out there?" he asked.

"Mr. Harry Thrall to see you."

"Send him in."

The young man grinned his way into the presence a few moments later. Spode recognized him as the sort that ladies like — possibly an advantage for a parking attendant. Not the sort he himself took to, however. He was perhaps 23, 24, slender, with intensely black hair slicked down with some art, and good features that shone with the conviction that, by golly, they *were* good, weren't they? They supported an insinuating manner, easy and confident.

"Mr. Spode, sir? I'm Harry Thrall."

Spode extended his hand. He judged a man by the firmness of his handshake. Harry darted fingers into his hand, giving Spode a sensation of warmth that had him suppressing a shudder as they sat down.

"My father said to give you this."

"Thank you," said Spode, rocking forward to take the proffered envelope. Opening it, he read:

```
Dear Bob:

    This accompanies my son Harry. I
am grateful for your assistance, and
stand personal surety as to Harry's
ability and energy.

    If ever I might be of service to
you, do not hesitate to contact

                    Your humble servant,
                    Vergil Thrall
```

Spode couldn't help snorting. Thrall was a capable contractor, and he felt every confidence his Tower would not soon be toppling over, but that any return of services might be required wasn't likely.

"Well, well," he said. He did not care for Harry's

handshake. Nor for his manner. Nor for his person. But Harry, he thought, would have his uses. Everyone has his uses. "Glad to be of help. Your father's in good health, I trust?"

"Oh yes, sir."

"Please give him my regards.

"Well, I imagine he told you what we have in mind for you? We have a parking garage over on Fifth Avenue—Fifth and Jeff Davis: The Spiral. That's two blocks upriver, one block south. Go over there and see Charlie."

"Sure thing, Mr. Spode." Harry smiled, the shift of his jaw forming dimples. *Dimples!* "Thank you, sir."

## 3.

THE SPIRAL GARAGE was only a five-minute walk from the Spode Tower, but it took Harry several hours to arrive.

First he returned to River House, his hotel, the best in Falls City (and another Spode property). He hoped to see again the maid who showed him memorable kindness upon his arrival the previous afternoon.

Unfortunately, she wasn't on duty. The difficulty was that, consulting his wallet over breakfast, Harry found that the temptations he succumbed to on his arrival—even on a Sunday evening, Falls City offered an illicit saloon that lubricated his way to a poker table—had put it into an embarrassing condition, and he needed assistance in removing his suitcase from the hotel, as he had no money to pay his bill.

So he returned and freshened up, and had the extraordinary good fortune of making the acquaintance of one Miss Etta when she knocked on his door to make up his room. The fetching Miss Etta proved amenable to his suggestion that they improve their acquaintance.

The upshot was that Harry strolled out of the dining room after lunch, having signed the meal to his room, stopped at the desk to extend his stay another night and darted up the alley to find his suitcase behind a trash can, just where Miss Etta said it would be, and carried it off with him to the Spiral Garage. Too bad for her, she also loaned him a dollar, which meant she wouldn't be seeing him again.

A prophecy of Frank Lloyd Wright's Guggenheim Museum, the Spiral Garage was a pioneering structure built in 1919, the creation of a cranky old architect named J.J. Gaffney. Its concrete ramps spiraled to a height of 30 feet, branching off to floors that accommodated 25 automobiles each.

Patrons dropped off their cars at the entrance and went on their way. Charlie or another attendant would park them upstairs—driving past Mr. Spode's cream-colored Packard in its niche just inside the entrance—and return downstairs at the double via the manlift, a continuously moving cable: grab the cable and step onto one of the chocks fitted into it and fly downwards. When a patron returned, the attendant flew aloft like an angel on the upwards cable to fetch the car again.

Though business wasn't what it was in the Twenties, solo lunchtime duty ran Charlie off his feet. So when Harry appeared, he gave him the big hello, put him into blue coveralls and demonstrated the easy trick of stepping onto the manlift. Eyeing the suitcase, he also told him about Mrs. Good's boarding house farther down Jeff Davis, promising she would offer credit until payday.

Harry's sole disappointment that day was the scarcity of tips. Men felt a nickel was ample, however dismayed his expression at sight of the lowly coin. And the ladies, instead of tipping, let their eyes go out of focus as they screwed their lips into a smiling, *"Thank you."*

Still, at day's end as Harry rode the trolley down Jeff Davis beside his suitcase his pocket was jingling with 60 cents.

## 4.

MRS. GOOD, CHARMED by him — and by his father's personal acquaintance with Robert Spode, Jr. — gave Harry a comfortable room and promised patience with the rent.

Falls City, it turned out, suited Harry. Work at the Spiral Garage involved little that resembled labor. Washing cars came closest, but on a fine day, with sun flooding the bay where he did that task, even that was easy, particularly with young women passing by and taking notice of his taking notice of them.

After work he pursued them at the movies — he loved movies — or in the parks or at the vaudeville theaters down Third Avenue. Soon he had a favorite tavern or two. After the season opened, on his days off he attended games of the city's minor-league baseball team, *The Night Riders.*

And soon he was undertaking daily explorations of the countryside. The midafternoon doldrums were his boss's naptime, when Charlie would set his office door ajar and lean against it in such a way that his feet were visible, alertly positioned under the desk, but anybody opening it would wake him up before he could be seen to be sleeping.

That became Harry's time to borrow cars for a quick look around Falls City and its environs.

One afternoon he was driving a Plymouth along Falls Road, which hewed close to the river beneath bluffs surmounted by great houses. Flowering trees — pear, apple and cherry, dogwood in white or pink — brightened the riverbank.

A yellow Auburn Phaeton convertible rushed up behind him and with a blare of its horn swerved past. The glimpse he got told him only that the driver was a young woman. She half raised her hand in passing, but stopped the motion when, Harry guessed, she realized the Plymouth's driver was not who she expected to see.

Stepping on it, he drew abreast.

"Thought I knew you," he called over from the other lane. *"Sorry!"*

Slowing up, she frowned at him — frowned very prettily beneath her bell-shaped hat. But the frown relented at his steady smile; her blue eyes widened and she giggled.

"Thought *you* were Edna Chance."

"She drive a car like this?"

*"Very* like," she returned. "You steal it?"

"Who wants to know?"

"You must be new here," she called.

"Just washed it for her," Harry said, "back at the Spiral Garage."

"Oh *really?"* she said, her voice sliding up an octave. "Did Daddy hire you?"

"That depends. Who's your Daddy?"

Laughing, she accelerated, in front of him making a squealing, two-wheeled turn through gateposts bearing a wrought-iron arch that spelled *Overridge.*

Next afternoon, returning downstairs on the manlift, Harry saw ascending on the other cable a woman! A petite young beauty who, equally startled to see him, still had the wit to shift her weight from one hip to the other and flash a naughty look.

Leaning out to look up her dress, Harry heard her laugh.

At the bottom he stepped across and flew upwards in her wake. Too late. He got back to earth again as the Auburn turned onto Fifth Avenue amidst honks and screeching brakes.

He woke up Charlie.

"Charlie, Charlie— Who's the girl drives the Auburn?"

"She here?" said Charlie, leaping to his feet.

"No, just left. Got her car herself."

"Everything OK?"

"Yeah, sure. Just wondered who she is."

Charlie sat down again.

"That's Mr. Spode's girl Lucie—Lucie Spode White?"

"So she's married?"

"*Yeah,* she's married. Married a White."

"Is that good?"

"Boy next door," Charlie said noncommittally. "Old lumber family. See a guy driving along in a fire truck shiny as an apple, that's him—his hobby. But look, her Daddy don't like her parking her car by herself or riding the cable, so next time you see her, stop her."

"Sure thing."

Charlie sighed, re-positioning his door.

"Then again, she's got a mind of her own, that one."

"That's the idea I got, seeing her," replied Harry.

## 5.

FAR THE RICHEST man in Falls City—having become so as a young man, but even richer now that he's also the oldest—is rolling down the gravel paths of Indianola Farm in a Bath chair. Sitting in the sun morning and afternoon are the highlights of his day. He says nothing, however, for strokes have left him mute.

Ever since little Bobby Spode—Robert Spode, Sr.—marched his 18th Volunteers home from bloody victory at Chickamauga (slaveholders the Spodes may have been, but they stood with the Union), it was said of him that he had his fingers in everything.

After slavery ended, Bobby Spode pushed with Northern energy to exploit the landscape surrounding Falls City, and took a great fortune out of it, even as his cohorts gave themselves up to the drinking of juleps, ,nostalgic for the old times when their fields rang with slaves' singing. Postwar Falls City relaxed into a slower, actually more Southern stance than it presented before what local ladies still delicately referred to as "the late unpleasantness."

But then, its founding families were Virginian in origin, younger sons who pushed across the Alleghenies to transplant an even more gracious version of Old Virginia than Virginia itself could any longer afford them.

They claimed the Qwattata Valley—*Qwattata* an Indian word variously translated as "dark and bloody ground" or "heart of darkness"—and built it into a secret kingdom (or a lost one; geography helped preserve its relative isolation). The hemp and tobacco fields worked by their slaves gave them wealth, enabling them even after Emancipation to devote so much thought and care to their way of life that, in a way otherwise unknown to the world, save perhaps in Japan, it came to consume as well as to define them.

The local joke had it that Falls City was named for the Fall of Man, the lamentable state of its morals and wide-open character of its amusements advanced as proof.

In fact, its lapsarian name derived from the Falls of the Qwattata River. The sole interruption to navigation between Pittsburgh and New Orleans, for a half-mile they lash the slow Qwattata to rapids over a rocky drop of 30 feet.

From earliest times the Falls necessitated the transshipment of cargo along the shoreline. Falls City came into being to take advantage of the fact, roosting there like a highwayman above a turnpike: He *will* be paid. He *will* take his cut.

After the Falls City Canal was built, shunting river traffic clear of the rocks, transshipment was no longer necessary. But the city still collected its toll; rather, the Falls City Canal Co. did.

Bobby Spode built that canal. The idea for it was old, the need obvious, but it was Robert Spode, Sr., scion of prosperous local planters, who acted on it. After his return from the Civil War, young Captain of the local Union regiment, he conjured up the necessary funds by every scheme and dodge a fertile mind not overburdened with honesty could devise, and never faltered through the difficulties of completing the work.

Once gouged through rock, the canal gushed money for the city and region—and especially for him. And by selling the quarried limestone detritus cheap, he insured that Falls City rose dignified and handsome.

Miss Willis, the new nurse, pushes the Bath chair in the strengthening April sun.

She's a blooming girl of 20. The Old Man, his hairless head wobbling atop a wizened chicken neck, doesn't know how long she'll stay. Most don't stay long, for he *will* put his fingers where they don't belong. And whenever the girls leave, old Mrs. Shea comes back to make his life a misery until a new nurse is hired. Mrs. Shea is ill-favored and ill-tempered, red in the face, as loud as she needs to be, and brooks no nonsense.

But pretty Lily Willis hasn't yet proved herself

uncomplaisant.

She finds the garden that he favors, protected by hedges. He licks his dry lips. She positions him in the sun and takes the end of a stone bench beside him. Through the balustrades she watches the foaling meadow, where fine colts graze and run with their mothers.

The Old Man leans into her. A crablike hand grazes her shin, as if by accident.

She slaps it away.

He will not be deterred. Robert Spode, Sr. gets what he wants, and always has done. *Always*.

But Miss Willis can choose. She has a job, a good one for a time when none can be found. And he happens to know—she's told him, some nurses talk out loud as though he's an old dog incapable of understanding—that her father and brothers are out of work, her sister crippled. She's the breadwinner for four, living expense-free away off here in the room next to his (but, providentially for her, up three steps).

So she needs the job, but if it doesn't suit her, she can leave. It's a free country.

He sends his hand crawling back up her leg, while libidinous eyes drill her, present her with her alternatives. It takes time, but he lodges his fingers. Miss Willis, upset, looks away, while the Old Man, trembling, closes his eyes and brings the thumb of his other hand to his mouth, licking it like an all-day sucker.

## 6.

A FEW WEEKS after arriving in Falls City, Harry finally laid eyes on Lucie's husband.

A charity ball was taking place at the River House. The Spode Packard went home as usual promptly at 5:00 o'clock, but at 7:30 Spode, accompanied by his wife, returned downtown in the rear of a grand old Minerva. His liveried chauffeur commanded the uncovered front compartment. His daughter and her husband followed in their chauffeured Cadillac.

Harry worked overtime helping to park guests' LaSalles and Lincolns in a shuttle operation between hotel and garage, catching glimpses of high-life as he did so. The Spode drivers and others passed several hours in Charlie's office playing gin and drinking bourbon. Late in the evening the shuttle reversed direction, and Harry started delivering cars to the River House curb. The chauffeurs put away their cards, shared packets of Sen-Sen and went off to pick up their charges.

Harry happened to be dropping off an Imperial when Robert Spode, Jr. pushed out through the revolving door. Immediately behind him strode a woman in a fall of black silk broken only by ranks of diamonds worn like medals for long service. They said nothing to each other. Obviously she was his wife.

Next out the door tripped Lucie Spode White in a more colorful if daringly diaphanous confection. The squiffy tuxedo behind her stumbled, getting slapped in the rear by the door.

While Spode summoned the Minerva, Squiffy Tux made an extra revolution, helplessly shrugging his shoulders, even looking a little panicky as the door pushed him around again. Lucie meanwhile rose up stern next to her mother, pulling at her pearls as though she wished to throttle the man. Her father laughed good-naturedly, the couples that piled up behind tittered, too, and sidewalk spectators guffawed. But Lucie pressed her lips tightly together in just the way her mother did.

The hapless figure who finally cleared the door was Pearl Gossamer White. Although it sounds to Northern ears an odd name for a man, south of the Mason-Dixon line *Pearl* is a perfectly respectable man's name. Losing his hair and putting on weight, Lucie's husband was fully ten years older than she, and twice her size.

Funny world, Harry thought, trotting back to the Spiral, when a girl like that ends up with a mug who can't even get himself through a door.

# 7.

A FEW DAYS later, Harry was smoking at the garage entrance while Charlie caught 40 winks. Though barely May, a foretaste of the jungle humidity that rots Falls City in the summertime was squatting over it. The Auburn roared in. Harry stood in its way, but had to jump sideways quick.

"That's OK, Miss Spode, I mean Mrs. White," he said. "I'll take care of it."

Lucie gave him a balked look, but said nothing, got out and hurried up Fifth Avenue on high heels. Harry's crotch lumped as he watched.

He drove the Auburn up and around to the top level and left it at the farthest, darkest spot there. Did it by instinct. He had no plans. Harry was no plan-maker.

Checking to see that Charlie still slept, he repaired to the toilet and washed his face and combed his hair. Gave himself a good look in the mirror.

And got a good look back: Looking *good*.

Charlie woke up cranky, as always, and hustled Harry around to wash and wax a Studebaker. Accidentally, Harry soaked the front of his coveralls, and came close to telling Charlie what he could do with his job.

Charlie yelled, *"Harry!"*

Harry appeared, wet down his front, a walking reproach to management.

"Harry, get Mrs. White's car," Charlie said, and jumped on the cable to fetch another customer's. Lucie stood by, her expressionless eyes on the clinging front of the coveralls.

Harry gave her a very frank look.

She returned it. Without breaching the lacquer of her surface—only melting it a little—appetite glowed like a breathed-on chunk of charcoal. Harry wiped his hands and grabbed the cable without looking at her.

She was right behind.

At the top he leapt off and made for the Auburn, keeping ahead of her steps clicking briskly on the concrete. Led her there and opened the passenger door. She got in and he pushed the Bakelite lever that dropped the seatback. He was getting on top of her when her splayed fingers stopped him.

"Get that wet thing *off!*" she commanded.

He took off his coveralls while she snapped her pocketbook open and withdrew a foil. He presented himself and she deftly unrolled the lambskin on him, then lay back, hiked up her dress and grimaced as he tore her underwear aside and entered her. Within moments—she as energetic as he—they had the springs squeaking in a frantic rhythm.

When it ceased, Lucie looked at her diamond-faced watch.

"Oh shit," she said.

She got out momentarily to pull down and smooth her dress and repair her face (looking *good*, she noticed; but then nothing so nourishes the skin). Harry could have said something, but didn't, and she was not there to elicit his conversation. Men have their limits, she was all too familiar with them. Their uses, too, of course.

It amused her, taking the wheel, to put out her hand. He took it and didn't squeeze; only held it while producing his set of dimples.

She laughed with great good cheer, and rushed her car down the ramp and into the street, so recklessly a delivery truck sideswiped a bus.

As for Harry, he had no idea what had happened, but he definitely liked it.

## 8.

LUCIE SPODE WHITE'S upbringing was the most proper that money could buy. An only child, she was educated at home by an English governess until the age of nine, when she entered the Falls City Female Seminary. At 17 she graduated to a life of charitable pursuits.

Yearbook photographs display her developing self. At nine, Lucie's an ethereal creature with a gauzy, indistinct gaze. Even lined up with dewy classmates similarly wreathed in Alice-in-Wonderland tresses, Lucie projects a pixie-like set-apartness. An observer trembles to turn the page lest he find her name gracing a monument of weeping cherubs in Heaven's Mead, the cemetery her grandfather laid out in waste land not otherwise developable.

But Lucie thrives. As she enters her teenage years, personality begins to emerge from beneath her great golden arc of hair. She peers out frankly. Soon she bobs that hair, and pins her uniform so as to show some leg and bring her bosom — more full than the age's ideal — to prominence.

Her classmates continue to vie in the eternal sweepstakes for best little girl, but Lucie looks Photoshopped from the future into the antique pictures. Her gladness of the flesh is irresistible. She appears to have figured out some things. First — for sure — that she's heiress to the richest family around. Second, whether through reading Poe's *The Purloined Letter* or through instinct alone, she discovers how invisible fearlessly open behavior can be.

Henceforth her openness alternately shocks and amuses, while always misdirecting attention. People's eyes light up at mention of Lucie's latest saying, even as no one seems to realize that her flamboyant language is no pose adopted for effect, but that her speculation in august company about a waiter's endowments signals her intended investigation of same, or that her lauding the charms of a River House porter is based on personal knowledge.

After she marries, this hypersuggestiveness of talk that never sleeps begins to wear on her husband, especially since she seldom sleeps with *him*, but he never realizes that her ready account of seeing the most handsome devil walking down Jeff Davis is her self-absolving mode of confessing that later she did a crazy thing with that devil at the Falls City Overlook. *The Purloined Letter*, together with the French letter, gave Lucie all the freedom a cultivated young lady could wish.

In her last class pictures, a French letter already secretly resides in her pocketbook. Representing perfect possibility, her prized possession — acquired from her best friend's brother —

radiates powerfully from its small square foil. It primes her, arms her, makes her as tense and self-aware as though she carries a vial of nitroglycerine the least knock might explode, to leave her but a smoking crater in the landscape.

In the event, it becomes a wearisome possession, too, for it's not until almost her 17th birthday that she tears it open. The Spodes are at their 30-room summer cottage in Harbor Creek, Michigan, when, perusing newspaper stock-market tables on the porch, her grandfather suffers his first stroke. In the confused aftermath, even as the Old Man, propped up in bed, is fixing his family with an angry gimlet eye, Lucie allows the caretaker's son to comfort her in the attic.

Thereafter her supply of condoms is assured; she requires them of her boyfriends as the price of admission.


# 9.

ONE DAY IN MAY Harry was tabulating his troubles as he scrubbed a Marmon's fender.

Charlie was making him wash more and more cars but, judging from the dribble that came Harry's way, pocketing most of the tips. And on the home front, there were tensions with his landlady and her medieval standards.

Why did Mrs. Good rent to both sexes if she was against their getting to know each other? It was embarrassing to be threatened with eviction for being found in the room of Mrs. Brown—40 if a day, a motherly sort plying him with cookies because that's what women of 40, their own lives over, *do*.

They were sitting on a couch separated by a plate of said cookies when Mrs. Good burst in and at the top of her lungs ordered Harry back where he belonged *"or else,"* and further informed Mrs. Brown that she ought to be ashamed of herself.

Now on a Wednesday at 1:00 o'clock, he had hours to go before — before *what,* going home to more scolding from Mrs. Good?

The Auburn darted into the Spiral and up the ramp. Harry leapt for the cable.

"Harry, come back here!" Charlie yelled. Harry ignored him.

The Auburn was poised at the top of the ramp, waiting. Lucie pushed the passenger door open. Harry got in and could hardly close it against the centrifugal force of their spiraling descent.

At the bottom it stopped.

"Charlie, you don't mind if I kidnap Harry for a little, do you?" Lucie purred.

"Well, now — " Charlie said.

"I want him to listen to my motor."

"Well, I guess it'll be all right, Miz White, just bring him back safe and sound."

"Oh, he'll be better than ever," she assured him, and sped into traffic. Harry heard a crash behind them.

"Engine sounds fine, ma'am," he said.

Laughing, she revved it. *"Thought* you liked how it goes," she said. "C'mon, want to have some fun?"

"Sure."

In the welter of Smoketown, the black neighborhood, she found Falls Road, and within minutes they were passing big brick and clapboard boxes set atop the bluffs.

"Who-all lives out here, anyway?" Harry asked.

"Newspaper," Lucie snapped, pointing to one house. "Falls

City *Truth?*" At the next, "Hartford Flour? One of the Hartford places. And there's Dad's, and there's mine."

They passed the matching white fences and great gates of Indianola Farm and Overridge. Harry glimpsed a columned white mansion and a rambling Jacobean manor.

"We're not going to your place?"

"*No.* Never *will* go to my place. Wouldn't be proper. That's Mr. White's house."

"Is he home?"

"And what's that got to do with the price of tea in China? I don't keep up with him. Might be home, might be at one of his timber camps. Whatever else you can say about the man, at least he owns timber all over the South. 'Course nobody's buying, so he comes home cross as a bear."

"Guess times are tough all over."

She glanced at him.

"You don't talk like you're from around here?"

"I'm from Tennessee."

"*Tennessee?* What do you do down *there?*"

"Grew up. Went to Vanderbilt Law in Nashville."

"Car jockey with a *law* degree?"

"Didn't quite finish. Girl got pregnant, seemed a good idea to go away for awhile."

She laughed long and loud.

"So where we going?" he asked.

"Someplace we can take our clothes off."

Turning off Falls Road, they swept through the countryside, passing several fine old inland houses, each commanding a green swath of land from atop a knoll. Short of Fontainebleau they turned into a collection of cabins behind a sign reading *Commonwealth Tourist Camp.*

Lucie put on the brake and dark glasses, dipped into her handbag and withdrew a $20 bill, which she folded and refolded and handed to Harry, saying, "We're Mr. and Mrs. Smith. Don't forget my change."

Harry stepped into the office, paid over the $20, signed the register *Mr. and Mrs. Smith,* received $17 in change and came out with the key to cabin No. 4.

"This way, dear," he called, and Lucie moved the car down the line and joined him indoors. The room was furnished with only a bed and hooks on the back of the door, its walls roughly plastered lathing.

As a concession to the proprieties of the situation, she sent him out to fetch the empty suitcase she happened to have in the Auburn's trunk. The trunk opened and closed with the sound of a hound dog's yawn.

"My change?"

He counted out $15.

"Two-dollar tip?" she said. "That for them or for you?" She wasn't pleased but said, when he produced the $2, "No, keep it, I insist. Yours if you earn it. You must think I'm made of money, everybody does, but it's not true."

"They tell me that between them, your Daddy and Granddaddy own half the state," Harry said.

"True," she said, sitting on the bouncy bed and taking off shoes and stockings. *"They* do, and I *don't.*"

She was still waiting, after all, at the bottom of the funnel down which the money must eventually come rattling. Her father stopped her allowance at her marriage, and the Crash shortly afterwards did her no good at all, for her husband cut her pin money — her only income — in half.

Poverty had a deplorably straitening effect on her; like somebody starving, she was monomaniacal, intent upon the one thing only. Later on she'd be *rich rich rich*. But later on is always later on.

"Harry, you probably have more cash money on you at any

given moment than *I* do. What my husband gives me? 'There's a Depression on,' he keeps saying. So tiresome. Don't have anything of my own until I turn *30*."

She said it as though 30 lay an eternity away. She was 25.

"Poor little rich girl," mocked Harry.

Looking at him, she said, "Get on with it, Bub."

He was happy to oblige. He stripped off his shoes and coveralls, was standing there naked when she disencumbered her head from her dress.

"My, my," she said as she unfastened her bra.

"Not so bad yourself," Harry replied, surprised at the fullness of her unleashed breasts. Leaning back, she pulled the covers out from under her. She was unexpectedly ample in the ass, too.

Reaching over, she withdrew a condom from her purse, ripped the package open and expertly unrolled it on him. In dulling his color and flattening his contours, there was something in the procedure akin to wrapping day-old fish. But it was the price of admission.

He entered — she had no use for preliminaries — and saw her face undergo a change, an inward arrest of attention, which intensified and deepened until — the bed squeaking insanely — together they burst jaggedly and loudly.

When they had their breath back she said, "Mr. Thrall, the State of Tennessee taught you how to treat a girl right."

"Wish I knew about you Falls City girls before now."

"So I'm a typical Falls City girl? Where do you live, anyway?"

"Memphis—"

"Here."

"Mrs. Good's boarding house, Jeff Davis and 16th."

"One room?"

"One room, Confederate generals on the wall, bathroom

down the hall. Dinner if I pay extra. No visiting the lady boarders in their rooms — strictly enforced. Lights out 10:00 o'clock, 11:00 on Friday and Saturday, *9:00* on Sunday."

Lucie laughed.

"Just wish you had a place," she said. "A little house of your own."

"Know of any?"

"No."

"Couldn't afford it anyway, on what your Daddy pays me."

"That's a shame," she said. "Hand me my pocketbook."

She took out another rubber, and they went at it again, but this time he turned her over, and soon, what with the headboard's chattering against the wall, a fine rain of plaster dust was powdering her back.

Harry's shift was over by the time they were finished with each other. There was no use rushing back to the Spiral. She dropped him off at an Interurban stop and, after riding the trolley downtown, he walked home the rest of the way with a snap to his wrists, whistling.

## 10.

CHARLIE WAS GRUFF and stone-faced the next day. If he wanted to know how Mrs. White's motor was running, Harry was prepared to boast that he got it to purr, all right, all right. But Charlie said nothing until Stan the night man was changing into his coveralls in the toilet.

"That Miz White," Charlie said out of the blue, not looking at Harry. "She's a fine lady. Thoroughbred. Best we got, and it's not for the likes of us to question her ways."

"*Huh?*"

"She's a handful, always has been," Charlie said. "First to her Daddy, and now to her husband."

"That the truth?"

"Stay away from her, Harry," Charlie said. "My last word."

Harry didn't like being chastised for pleasing a girl. Let Charlie worry about whose daughter she was. Let her *Daddy* worry. Let her *husband* worry, or polish his fire engines, or whatever he was used to doing after five years of being married to her.

It was a week before the Auburn came by the Spiral Garage again, and Harry didn't see it when it did. Charlie reluctantly came to find him, saying, "Miz White wants you."

Indeed she did. She was idling at the curb, dark glasses on, hat pulled low.

"How 'bout it, Harry? Have three bucks?"

He dug into his pocket.

"Paid rent yesterday. Got 75 cents to my name, Lucie, and it's got to last till Friday."

"Shit," she said. Pulling away, she was gone.

A few days later when she parked at the Spiral to go shopping, Harry confronted her on an upper level.

"Lucie, don't treat me like I'm something you point at in the butcher's window. I'm poor, but I can hold my own. I just don't have the money to —"

"That's just it, Harry, *exactly* the problem. It's fun and all that, but Pearl expects his $100 a week to pay for everything from stockings to gasoline — *everything* — and he won't give an inch. So I can't either."

Her heels tap-tapped towards the cable.

Harry called, "They tell me it's $20 million."

"Oh, I hope it's more than *that*," she scoffed over her

shoulder. Seized by the injustice of it all, she turned and lamented, hands on hips, "But I can't lay my mitts on *one thin dime* of it. One beau? Robbed a gas station just to spend a weekend with me. I gave him the idea — but I didn't think he'd *do* it!" She laughed at the memory. "But that was a time, I'm telling you."

"What happened to him?"

"I'm sure he still thinks it was worth it." She came up close and reached for Harry's crotch. "Real gentleman. My name never came up."

"That's just crazy."

Her hand was kneading bread. Which rose. He touched her, too.

"Jesus," she said. "Jesus, not *here*. OK, come on."

They hopped in the Auburn, Harry taking the wheel and gunning it down the ramp past Charlie's, "Cut it out, Harry, you don't have time —" and into the streets.

Her hand pushed them right. "Turn here."

They squealed onto a parkway.

"There's a place in Welshman's Park, at least it's free."

A few minutes later they parked beside a pavilion that overlooked a field of daisies. Bringing a blanket and her purse, they went down a path to a beech grove beside a stream, spread the blanket between big rocks, and went at it.

After the first bout Harry said, "You know, this is crazy."

"Broken record," said Lucie.

"I know, but— *Cheez*, here we are, hot for each other, but we don't have two nickels to rub together, no place to go."

"Harry, I have an idea. What we could do. *If* you have the balls."

Harry guided her hand below to weigh and assess.

"*Hmmm*, just maybe," she said. "Came to me back when the poor Lindbergh baby was kidnapped. Knew right off that if they kidnapped *me*, Daddy would pay a ransom of—well, of anything at all to get me back safe."

"Lucky kidnappers."

She sighed. Men *are* slow.

"We'd split it. Say it's a hundred thousand. How long would it take you to spend $50,000, Harry? That's more than most men make their whole lives. You could buy a house and car, put the rest in the bank and live off the interest. Be on Easy Street."

Harry's mouth fell open as he looked at her. Was she serious?

"More like, *you'd* be on Easy Street, *I'd* be on Death Row."

"No, Harry, there's no risk, 'cause I'm in on it with you. Won't catch us in the first place—I'm too smart for 'em—we *both* are—but if they *do*, there's no crime: Can't be kidnapping if it's the so-called victim's idea. They couldn't *do* anything to you, and that's if the *worst* happens. *And* we'd have fun in the meantime."

Men, when they think at all, do so at their own pace, and Lucie was used enough to the phenomenon to suppress her impatience. She reached to caress one of the small ears curled into his skull that reminded her of lapdogs' tails.

"See, Harry, my cut would get me to my inheritance. One trust fund comes when I'm 30, the big one when I'm 35."

He was still looking at her.

"*Fifty thousand dollars*, Genius," she said with asperity. "Have to figure it out, though, every detail. No point getting caught."

"So you have a plan?"

"No, I have the *idea*," Lucie answered. "The *plan* is your department. Work it out yourself, and don't tell me, don't say anything at all, 'cause if they figure out I'm in on it, no one gets *anything*."

Harry tore his eyes off her and, lying back on his arms, looked up through the leaves, bough lifted against bough in veils that obscured the bright sky beyond, and considered.

He was hooked. She knew it.

"When do you want — ?"

"Surprise me, Harry," Lucie said, revisiting her handbag. "*Astonish* me. And in the meantime, please fuck hell out of me."

As always, Harry did as he was told.

# 11.

THEIR AFFAIR CONTINUED hot for another two months.

There was no more talk of kidnapping — Lucie wouldn't allow it — though one day Harry, parking a phone-company truck, with absolutely nothing in mind relieved it of a shirt hanging in the rear and some wire and tools. As funds allowed they went back to the Commonwealth Tourist Camp, or rented rooms at a dubious tavern near the canal locks or at a certain notorious rooming house overlooking the train yards. A few times they returned to Welshman's Park.

At Lucie's bright-eyed insistence, one night Harry even smuggled her into his room at Mrs. Good's. It was an exciting if nerve-wracking hour, doing what they always did but in whispers, trying to dampen proclamations from the floorboards and bedsprings, stifling laughter and groans.

Afterwards, disaster threatened when, sneaking Lucie downstairs again, they ran smack into Harry's cookie-baking neighbor, stealthily heading for his room with a plate of warm Toll House. A ferocious scene ensued *sotto voce* and, though in the end Harry was somehow able to fix things up, for days Mrs. Good exclaimed at finding cookie crumbs and chocolate smears in her stair carpet.

Harry pressed for a reciprocal visit to Overridge, but Lucie turned the idea down flat. It was insulting. Harry preened himself on being her secret lover, but their relationship existed solely on her terms. Him it took into account only as a tool of her indulgence.

Generations of Spodes before her had done the same, of course; it was a function of social aspiration in Falls City that no one ever looked askance at what the Spode girls or boys might be up to, how they were risking their social standing by flouting standards of behavior: There was no risk. Harry grew to resent it, especially as the affair kept his pockets as empty as Lucie's purse.

But it was Charlie who took the decisive step. By the end of June he felt so frazzled with the responsibility of knowing what the boss's daughter was up to, so fearful of blame should husband or father cotton to what was going on—and was losing out on so many naps—that he fired Harry.

"Hate like hell to do it, Harry, you're not a bad fellow and times are hard," he said. "But you just can't work at a job like it's something you do in between paying attentions to a lady friend."

"Not me, Charlie, it's *her*, that's the way—"

"And I warned you, too. So I'm letting you go."

"Letting me *go?*" Harry smiled at the idea. "I don't think Mr. Spode will—"

"Told him already. Oh, I kept *her* name out of it. Told him I caught you driving Mrs. Prettyman's Reo back in from one of your joyrides the other day. He was *shocked*."

"Well, let me tell him I'm fucking his daughter, see what he says *then*."

"Get out, Harry. And with talk like that, you'd best go back to Tennessee."

"I fucking well will!"

Harry walked the whole way home. Felt calmer by the time he got there, for all that sweat soaked his shirt. Thought he'd give Lucie a call.

There was a phone beside the stairs. He put in his nickel and dialed 3, the single digit a relic of her grandfather's founding the Qwattata Valley Telephone Company 50 years earlier.

"Hello, may I speak to Mrs. White, please?" he asked.

"Miz White ain't home," said a woman in a rich African timbre. "Who should I say called?"

He gave his name and dictated the boarding house's number, and the rest of the evening chased fellow boarders away from the phone. But Lucie didn't call.

The next day Harry dressed up and went to the Spode Tower. Miss Bryant permitted him to sit in the outer office, but paid him no mind as she gravely sorted the mail.

Spode strode in on the dot of 10:00.

"Hello, Thrall," he said. He didn't offer his hand. "Bad business over at the Spiral. Charlie told me."

"Yes, sir, it was a bad thing to do, and I apologize and won't ever—"

Spode was already moving towards his door.

"Well, Thrall, if you learned anything from it, that's all any of us—"

"But Mr. Spode, sir, I *need* that job, sir. I'll be good after this."

"Should have thought of that before," said Spode, entering his office and closing the door so firmly its engraved glass rattled. Miss Bryant glared at Harry over the top of her glasses, impervious to his rueful offering of dimples.

Harry made himself saunter back to the elevator. As he waited, trefoil windows gave him a last grand view of Falls City's limestone growth catching the morning sun, with the Falls boiling furiously below.

When the elevator arrived and its red-coated attendant muscled open the doors, Harry, head down, started to get on.

Derisive, but familiar, laughter backed him up.

"Falls City manners, sir, are to let the lady *off* first," Lucie said.

"Lucie!"

"Thank you, Patrick," said Lucie, frozen-faced. The operator closed the doors and the cab dropped from sight.

"Lucie, I lost my job," Harry said.

"Careless of you," she returned. "Times like these."

"I—I— Do you have ten bucks you could loan me?"

It wasn't even what he meant to say.

Lucie blushed and her eyes flashed. She snapped open her pocketbook, found a $5 bill in it, and threw it on the floor. Across the room Miss Bryant stood up in shock.

"For services rendered?" Lucie sneered.

She walked towards her father's office. Harry picked up the money and pressed the elevator button. He offered Miss Bryant a toothy, never-say-die smile.

But he realized that to Lucie he was nothing—nothing at all.

## II.   Four months later

## 12.

SUMMER BURNED THE Qwattata Valley, then burned itself out. It felt almost chilly the morning of Wednesday, October 10, when Harry Thrall drove to Falls City in his new wife's old Chevy coupé.

He pulled off the road at the Falls Overlook to smoke a cigarette. The black webbing of the railroad bridge and white girders of the auto bridge set off the city's stony mass. Harry thought that, with its deep-set windows, Falls City resembled an old man with his eyes closed. An old man who couldn't see what you were getting up to.

He flicked the butt away, took off his suit jacket — revealing a blue Qwattata Valley Telephone Co. shirt — got back behind the wheel, crossed the bridge and drove up Falls Road.

MISS WILLIS WAS shrouding the Old Man in a blanket and positioning him in the sun.

Unlike Harry, Miss Willis had kept her job. It was easier now that the weather was cooler and she could sit next to her charge with a blanket spread over both, the Old Man doing what soothed him with no one being the wiser. No one being the wiser, Miss Willis knew, is what matters. So she had dried her tears and put away any thought of starving her family rather than undergo the shame of caring for the Old Man. No one being the wiser, there was no shame.

So while the Old Man delved, peacefully nibbling his thumb and meditating a return to the womb, she watched the colts, already almost grown, frisking about.

THE OLD MAN'S SON sat in his office amidst a glitter of bronze and polished walnut, poring over the figures spread across his desk.

They were shabby, lifeless figures—and yet he detected a stiffening. The freefall of 1930, '31, '32 was arrested, the slight resistance that manifested itself in '33 possibly firming.

He looked at the clock. 10:30. Two more hours before he could make his processional to the Bandits Club for lunch.

Sighing, he went back to the numbers.

WHEN HER BLACK MAID, Bessie Longworth, brought in the tray at 9:00 o'clock, Lucie begged her to let her sleep.

No surprise to Bessie. Only the day before Mr. White had finally left—now that the heat was moderating—on a delayed tour of Alabama pine woods. Her mistress needed to recover from his unusually long stay at home.

To Lucie it was simply remarkable the way a husband on the premises weighs upon one's spirits. Under the covers she kicked just thinking about how Pearl, shunning his downtown office, preferred to stay underfoot at home. At least he was obedient about going off to play with his fire trucks. In fact, foreseeing how it might absorb additional time and attention, Lucie had suggested that he build a scale-model steam railroad across the grounds. His response was a little-boy look of big-eyed stupefaction. He liked trains, too.

But now he was gone. Not a moment too soon. And she was in the mood for adventure, if uncharacteristically at a slight loss as to how to proceed.

Perhaps they'd been too precipitous exiling what's his name — *Dimples* — last June. The lad who replaced him at the Spiral Garage came straight from the country. Lucie had no settled objection to country boys (quite the contrary), but this one was portly and missing teeth. She hated to touch her car after that bumpkin sat in it.

Who else was there? Well, she was not to the bottom of her list yet. But no one was in Dimples' league. There was that new waiter at the Bandits who recently served up a look along with her soufflé, and that welder at the Boat Works she met somewhere. Not to mention the new priest at St. Eustace's Episcopal Cathedral.

If need be, she could always go looking. Most any man in Falls City could be brought to worship at the altar of Lucie, and do it with instinctive, blood understanding of the rules of the game, the discretion required. Dimples broke the rules, simple as that. But *damn!* he was fun.

Sighing, she peeked at the clock. 10:45. If she wanted lunch anywhere she'd better think about getting a move on. But it was so pleasant just to lie there, tall windows open to the river flowing beneath her terrace and sunlight dancing across the room, picking out crystal and cloisonné and enlivening the Paul Plasche swimming-hole scene on the wall. Its robust nudes gave her hope at every glance. A girl needs hope.

Overridge was a gabled brick Jacobean house built so cleverly across the ridgeline one couldn't readily grasp how big it was. But it wasn't so enormous that Lucie, dozing again, didn't unconsciously pick up the tread and voice of a stranger, shortly after a car chugged up the long uphill drive.

She pressed a malachite button at her bedside and eventually Bessie, holding a feather duster in token of having been torn away from pressing duties, opened the door.

"Bessie, who's here?" Lucie asked, yawning.

"Telephone man, Miz White. Says there's trouble with the line."

And a man in a phone-company shirt squeezed past her into the room.

*Dimples!*

Lucie's mouth opened. She closed it again without saying anything, but couldn't suppress how her face lighted up.

Closing the door behind him, Harry forced Bessie's wrists together behind her back and marched her — yelping, "*Yi! Yi! Yi! Yi!*" — across to the dressing table and pushed her into the chair.

"What's he *doing*, Miz White? *Crazy* man."

"What *are* you doing?" Lucie demanded. "*Sir?*"

Saying nothing, Harry pulled wires out of his pocket — vulcanized-rubber telephone wires — and tied Bessie's arms to the chair. She started to scream, but he pushed a handkerchief into her mouth and she gagged instead.

"I said, what the *hell* do you think you're doing?" Lucie repeated, adding, as an afterthought, "And *who* the hell are you?"

Harry answered by taking a homemade blackjack — a length of pipe stuffed in garden hose — out of his pocket and approaching the bed. Avoiding her eyes, he yanked Lucie up — she was half-screaming in surprise and fear; *never* had she been treated thus — and slugged her with it.

"*Oww!*" she yelled. "*Shit*, that hurts!"

He made to hit her again, but she prized the pipe from his hands and threw it out a window. The gash in her scalp bled copiously. She pressed a pillow to it.

Taking a piece of paper from his shirt pocket and tossing it on the bed, Harry finally spoke.

"You're coming with me, Mrs. White. I have a gun, and if you resist or make any noise, I'll shoot. Shoot the both of you."

"All right," said Lucie. "Let me get dressed."

She crossed through her dressing room, where Bessie had laid out her dove-gray silk, disappeared into the bathroom and began to draw a bath.

"Ma'am, don't do that," Harry said, rattling the locked door. "Ma'am? There's no time for that."

"Be a jiffy!" Lucie called.

Harry was sitting on the bed gloomily watching Bessie— and Bessie was watching back—15 minutes later when Lucie, feeling much more herself, appeared. She looked ready to wheel the Auburn into town for lunch. Bending over her dressing table, she draped herself with pearls and matching earrings, then pinned her hat over the wet spot in her hair.

"Well, Mr. Telephone Company Man, now that you have me, what are you going to do with me?"

Checking her bonds, Harry admonished Bessie, "Tell them they want to see their darling daughter alive, pay the ransom. Or else."

"Hurry," said Lucie. "Let's go."

Harry scurried after her.


## 13.


THEY ENCOUNTERED NOBODY inside the house. Cook and butler were in the kitchen, awaiting Lucie's orders regarding lunch. The housemaids dusted, gossiping about the good-looking man from the telephone company. After Lucie led the way down the staircase and out the front door, two gardeners watched from a distance while Harry installed her in the coupé. He insisted she crouch on the floor under a blanket, and at first she did.

The gardeners didn't realize they were witnessing an abduction and, after a due interval leaning on their rakes, went back to work.

Henry turned the Chevy onto Falls Road and found the downtown bridge again. Recognizing the distinctive whirr of tires on its grating, Lucie popped up into the seat. She wanted to enter into the spirit of the thing, but started with a remonstrance.

"Didn't have to *hit* me, Harry. I'm still bleeding."

"Sorry, I *did* have to. Your colored woman saw me do it. Makes us safe."

"What did I say about your balls? But what if somebody sees me?"

"That's why you should stay on the floor."

"I will *not*, it's dirty."

"Then let's hope no one sees you."

"Here, I'll pull my hat down. You, too." She reached over. *"Now* you look like a gangster."

He grinned. "Do I?"

"Baby Face Harry. Of the Thrall Gang. Oh, Harry, this *is* fun. Where are you taking me?"

"Indianapolis."

"That'll take hours!"

He shrugged.

"C'mon, Harry, let's pull over first." Reaching over, she rubbed the part of him that usually made up his mind. "Pigeon Roost Massacre's ahead, that's a quiet place. And I've been *such* a good girl."

When they got there, they pulled off, jounced up a dirt road and parked beside an obelisk memorializing an Indian slaughter a century earlier. The tumulus made for a ready bed. Harry spread the blanket while Lucie stripped and snapped open her purse. His hand at first carried hers away from him, but hers insistently returned and she unrolled the lambskin on him.

Twenty minutes later, much refreshed, they were tooling north through rolling farmland. Lucie was still excited.

"Oh Harry, what larks! What a lovely day. Was that your ransom note? How much did you demand, $100,000?"

"Good round number, ain't it? Stuck in my mind."

"Oh, that's grand! How'd you say to send it?"

"Said to follow instructions from my intermediary."

"Intermediary!"

*Intermediary?* Her heart thudded.

"Sure. That's the hard part of the business, you know— getting the money without getting nabbed. Set up a ransom drop, nine times out of ten the G-Men catch you there. This way, our go-between gets it, no risk to us—none a-*tall*—and takes his time figuring how to get it to us." He turned, grinning. "Foolproof."

Lucie took off her hat so she could dab her handkerchief to the wound on her head. She apprehended that her first-rate idea was being executed by a second-rate intelligence. That it could fail. And already was out of her control.

"Who— Who's your intermediary?"

"My dad."

Horrified, she opened her mouth to demand, "Turn around this instant!" Instead she trilled a mirthless little laugh.

"But Harry, that's as good as telling them who you are!"

He shrugged again.

"Same difference. Dad'll get the money to us, and I'll be on my way. They'll never find me, and you'll be back in the bosom of your family, good as new, except *rich*. You'll have your inheritance early."

"That's right," said Lucie evenly, but her stomach kicked. She reminded herself that, at worst, she had no liability, for there was no crime — only the money was at risk.

*Only the money!*

"Really, Lucie, I thought it through. It's on my old man to work it out, but he will. Safety's the thing. Remember, guys who do what I'm doing? They get the Chair."

"I hope you're right, Harry."

"Bet on it."

But clouds took over the sky, and with the sun hidden, the air chilly again, Lucie shivered.

# 14.

BESSIE COULD NOT get herself untied. She had to stay in that chair. She was mad, but at least had time to try to plumb what she saw pass between the telephone man and her lady.

That her lady was a woman of affairs of course she knew. It was a mainstay of their hilarious ongoing colloquy that Bessie had Bertram, her husband — the dark, steady, slow man of all work — and Miz White her ever-changing boys.

Bessie had never seen Harry Thrall before, had no reason to associate him with the parking attendant she knew her mistress found such diversion with in the springtime, but she had no doubt, judging by her expression when he slipped into the room, that she and the man knew each other—odds were, in the Biblical sense.

And that introduced the astounding idea that what she witnessed wasn't the kidnapping it purported to be, but a put-up job.

She might know more if she could read the note lying on the bed. It tantalized her from ten unreachable feet away.

Obviously money would lie behind such a scheme, and since money was up there with sex as a staple of her lady's complaints, that didn't exactly let Miz White off the hook, either.

Bessie remained tied up until the butler complained to Bertram that no one had told Cook what to fix for lunch. Bertram was hungry, too. So naturally it was a man's growling stomach that led to the knock on Lucie's door past noontime and to Bertram's venturesomeness, when the only response was a series of muffled grunts, in cracking it open.

He cracked it, then swung it wide and gawked. Only then did he think to go in and pull the gag out of his wife's mouth.

"Well, *finally*, good for nothing!" Bessie erupted. "Leaving me up here all day while those *mens* have our lady, doing who knows *what* to her."

Bertram fumblingly untied her while she heaved and pulled. She stood up, almost falling over, but got herself over to the bed and read the piece of typewriting on it:

```
Mr. White, we have your wife.
You will not see her again until
you pay a ransom of one hundred
thousand dollars ($100,000). Do
not call the police or the
F.B.I. We are watching you.
Vergil Thrall of Memphis,
Tennessee is our intermediary,
```

```
      though he don't know it. Pay and
      we return your wife. Pay not and
      we bury the corpus delecti!
```

"My good Lord!" Bessie screamed. "Bert, call Mr. Robert." When she saw him trying to decide whether she meant Junior or Senior, she screamed again, *"Junior, stupid."*

And when he picked up the phone and waited, then tapped the receiver and waited again, then reported that it was dead, she said with double exasperation, "Then go next door, *idjut."*

## 15.

LUCIE'S FATHER WAS just capping lunch at the Bandits Club with a post-prandial sip. It was still a luxury since Prohibition's recent end to enjoy his own product, Willinger's Reserve Bourbon, leisurely in sight of the world.

When Prohibition came in, most sachems of spirits duly shut down their distilleries, scorning to launch bootleg ventures. As gentlemen, they retained only sufficient private stocks to mourn the Confederacy as needed.

But Robert Spode, Sr. went a different way: What use was Junior's marriage to the former Miss Sawtooth if it didn't put Senator Sawtooth in his pocket?

There were conferences with the distinguished gentleman, an understanding was reached, and the Senator successfully introduced an amendment to the Volstead Act exempting a certain class of distilleries from having to axe open their barrels, splash their contents into the sewers and fire their employees. This certain class—so stringently was the amendment worded that only eight distilleries in the country met its requirements—was allowed to continue to make bourbon, albeit for medicinal purposes only.

Hence Willinger's stayed in business—*just*—until Prohibition's repeal, when it found itself able to sell its inventory at advantageous terms and ramp up operations again years ahead of its competitors.

The son at the Bandits Club musing about his father's foresight could only hope the mute Old Man was savoring his last great coup.

He set his glass down with a *chink!* that brought over a waiter to pull back his chair. On the street, half a minute's work with a toothpick brought his Packard to the curb. Back at the Spode Tower he was dismissing the car when a lobby man ran out.

"Mr. Spode, your house just phoned!" he shouted. "They've kidnapped your daughter!"

WITHIN TEN MINUTES Spode was back in the Packard, sitting next to Falls City's Chief of Police, Walter Eckerdt, and being escorted to Overridge by two motorcycles and a radio car. Already Spode was annoyed by Eckerdt's repetition of, "If it's true, we better call in the Bureau."

"Walt," he said, "will you please shut up?"

"The Lindbergh Law takes it out of my jurisdiction, Bob."

"Walt!"

Eckerdt shut up. But he turned his hat this way and that in his lap the remainder of the trip.

Bessie Longworth met them in the hall at Overridge and marched upstairs with them to the scene of the crime. There with dismay they surveyed the bed with its bloody pillow and the chair draped with telephone wires.

"Where's Mr. White?" asked Chief Eckerdt.

"He's at the camp," said Bessie. "The timber camp in I don't know where."

"Alabama, I believe," said Spode. "I'll call him, Bessie, if you'll get the number from—"

"Can't," Bessie said composedly.

"Why the hell not?"

"Phone's not working. Man cut the wire or something."

"Oh, crap."

She gave a full—almost full—recitation of events, acting out the parts. Her audience was horrified but rapt. She watched their faces carefully. Recounting the man's entry into her lady's bedroom, she failed to mention only one thing: Lucie's glad look of recognition. She described the kidnapper as a "skinny white man from the phone company."

"Bessie, he was *not* from the phone company," Spode said. "Will you please stop saying that?"

"Well, *said* he was, sir. Wore the shirt. How do I know different?"

At last she pointed out the ransom note lying in the folds of bedding. Seizing it, Spode read it and collapsed heavily on the bed before handing the note to the chief.

Eckerdt read it out loud, pronouncing *one hundred thousand dollars* with the round-voweled reverence it deserved.

"We need a telephone," Spode announced, getting to his feet. "Next door!"

He returned to his car—Chief Eckerdt scrambling after—and directed it up a gravel lane to Indianola Farm, his own place next door.

Seized by a new fright, Spode first bellowed down the hall, "Chester! Is Father here? Is Father all right?"

His butler came running.

"Yes, sir, he's outdoors again with Miss Willis."

"Go get him. Bring him in the house, and put the men on

the grounds. Open the gun case, distribute rifles and shotguns." He shut Chester's mouth by adding, "Seems my daughter's been *kidnapped.*"

He then left word with his son-in-law, or at least with the timber office in Alabama. Fortunately his own wife was safely taking the waters in Virginia. He hung up to find Chief Eckerdt crushing his hat again.

"Well? *Well?*"

"I think we better call in the G-Men, sir."

"Yes, yes," said Spode.

"A hundred thousand dollars, Mr. Spode: It's a lot of money."

"It's a fortune, Walt, an absolute *fortune*. You have no idea."

"Guess I'm asking if you can do it?"

"You worry about the F.B.I., Chief. I'll worry about the ransom."

# 16.

JOE ALBRIGHT, 26 YEARS OLD, was lanky, fair-haired and pleasing to look at.

Also he was new in town. In Falls City that designation can last the remainder of a lifetime, but in fact Albright had arrived only six months earlier to run the local F.B.I. office — three rooms in the Federal courthouse furnished in battered government-issue desks and decorated with Wanted posters (but it was their Golden Age). A photograph of J. Edgar Hoover's bulldog features presided; its frame distinguished his face from those of the Wanted.

It was Joe's first Bureau assignment, and Falls City, he thought, was about as far away from Boston—he was a product of Boston College Law School—as it was possible to get.

When Chief Eckerdt's call came in, Joe was failing to rouse himself from an after-lunch lethargy. His burger never settled well. But the deeper cause of his malaise of mind and body—of the nascent roll of fat at his belly—was having too little to do. There was a terrible dearth of Federal crime in Falls City. Far too few bank robberies to make life interesting. And although the biggest Mob resort east of Hot Springs was the casino in French Lick, Indiana, a mere two-hour drive away, that was out of his jurisdiction.

So Joe spent his days keeping watch on the railroad and bus stations to see if any public enemies might try to slip into town. He was bored, and had as much time on his hands for regrets as a French Foreign Legionnaire.

Chief Eckerdt was terse on the phone.

"Joe, got something for you," he said. "Lucie Spode White— You *do* know who that is?" The chief reminded himself that Joe was new, and a Yankee to boot.

"Sure, Chief. Haven't met her, but I know who—"

"*Kidnapped.* She's missing, we got a ransom note, witness in the colored cook"—in the background Bessie hollered that she was *not* the cook—"and you better get out here to Overridge, pronto."

"On my way, Chief," Joe snapped.

Grabbing a form, he wrote, replete with teletype kisses:

```
ATTN DIRECTOR XXXXX LUCIE SPODE
WHITE DAUGHTER PROMINENT SPODE
FAMILY KIDNAPPED TODAY FROM HOME
OVERRIDGE XXXXX NOTIFICATION 2:17
XXXXX HEADED OUT XXXXX SUGGEST ADDL
MEN XXXXX ALBRIGHT
```

He slapped it on his secretary's desk and ordered, "Get that on the wire right away."

Reaching for his hat, he dashed out to his official black Ford V-8, and used every cylinder getting to Overridge.

This could be it. This could be the case to crack his career wide open — for once and all shut up those who had him lined up for the bond business.

Since high school he'd dreamed of joining Hoover in building up his Bureau at the Department of Justice. Not an easy road, and so far a bewildering organization to negotiate. Some of the requirements! Being photographed nude, front and back, was disconcerting (except his sister assured him they did that at Vassar, too). An image flashed into his mind from the initiation party Mr. Hoover hosted with Mr. Tolson. He didn't remember much about that night. Another stray image came to mind. Pursing his lips, Joe decided he didn't remember *any* of it.

He returned to the problem at hand.

Hadn't met Lucie, but he'd glimpsed her. Seen her to notice her. Seen her run her Auburn up the curb outside the River House and hurry inside powdering her face — altogether, behavior you saw only in ladies of the streets or the very upper crust

Clearly a fast one, that beauty, slick as anything.

## 17.

OVERRIDGE WAS ALREADY in chaos when Joe arrived. He had to honk his way through the gang of reporters at the gates.

No public announcement brought them—the family was instinctively inclined to silence—but a sizable city cannot on the instant redeploy its police force without its being noticed, and when that redeployment concerns the first family of the place, everybody knows everything instantly.

Joe identified himself, flashed his badge, briefly put up his hands at the behest of a plainclothesman pointing a shotgun, then, after a positive answer to a radioed inquiry, drove up the hill with a patrolman next to him.

"Nice place," he observed. The driveway rose through bursts of rhododendron to sweeping lawns that offered views of the Qwattata Valley. The red-brick manor house commanded the hill. In a nearby barn he glimpsed bright red fire engines.

His Ford crunched to a stop on the gravel, alongside half a dozen police cars and trucks from the telephone company. His escort relinquished him to a family retainer with a rifle who marched him inside the front door. There Joe was directed to a lofty living room cozy with couches and flowers. A radio played, low. Spode stood in front of a roaring fire tearing apart a cigar. Chief Eckerdt sat at a desk barking into a telephone, "Hello? *Hello?*"

"Ain't got it yet!" he reported and slammed it down. "Ah, here's the G-Man."

Joe crushed Spode's hand. Through the pain on the other's face he read trust and gratification.

"Special Agent Joseph Albright, sir. Glad to meet you, except under these—"

"Yes, yes," said Spode. "Thanks for coming out."

"Any more of you?" the Chief put in.

"More coming," Joe said. "Teletyped Washington. Now, what's going on?"

Chief Eckerdt drawled, "Well, it's like this—"

"Get Bessie," Spode barked. "She was there."

Bessie Longworth was fetched from the back of the house and placed on a couch near the fire.

"Now Bessie, tell this man what happened."

She started with the telephone man's arrival.

Joe interrupted.

"Why did you think he was from the phone company?"

"'Cause that's what he tell me, say he the phone man, plus he has the shirt and the screwdriver, and he goes right to the kitchen phone and opens it up. It don' work after that."

"I see."

"Then she ring for me, and he needs to check her extension, so I go in—"

"Where was she?"

"In bed. Feeling poorly. Husband's away, you know," Bessie explained. "And the phone man, he push in past me, and her eyes get so big."

"What did you make of that?" Joe asked.

Bessie studied the rug. "Din' make nothing of it," she said.

"And then what?"

"He hit her—hit her with his big gun—and she go, '*Oww!*' and he ties me up and tells her to get ready, and she takes a bath—"

"A *bath?*"

"—and they leave. She say, 'Hurry, let's go,' and they go."

"Mrs. Longworth, did Mrs. White recognize this man?"

"Yes," said Bessie. "No. How I know a thing like that?"

"What did he look like?"

She furnished the particulars of a dark, slender young man.

"What time did this happen?"

"Getting on for 11:00 o'clock, and I'm sitting there hungry, and it takes hours, just hours, for Bertram to come and get me."

Bessie showed him the scene of the crime, again reenacting

the deed. When they returned to the living room, the chief was crowing, "All _right!_ Phone's back!"

Spode demanded, "Well, Albright, what do you think?"

"May I see the ransom note?"

Eckerdt relinquishing it, Joe took it by one corner, read it and tucked it away.

"Do you know this Vergil Thrall?"

"Built my Tower downtown," Spode answered. "Contractor out of Memphis. Sent up his son last spring to work at the Spiral Garage, but the boy couldn't manage to keep his job more than ten or 12 weeks."

"The son's name?"

"Harry Thrall."

Joe wrote it down.

"What's Harry Thrall look like?"

With distaste Spode described a dark, slender young man.

"Did he know your daughter?"

"Certainly not!"

"Could he have met her? Encountered her?"

"Oh, I suppose he might have brought her her _car_ on occasion."

"Where is he now?"

"No idea. Now, sir, if he's our man, why in heaven's name would he name his own father?"

"For a better shot at the ransom, sir. Collecting ransom's risky business. Hauptmann could tell you all about that — going on trial for his life because he passed a few marked bills from the Lindbergh ransom. I'll tell Washington, suggest we bait a trap with Mr. Vergil Thrall to catch our man and bring your daughter home."

"Do it," said Spode.

"I'll be back," Joe told him, and left.

The chief was busy answering the phone. No sooner did he

set it down than it rang again.

"Keep the line clear," he barked into it and hung up. It rang again instantly. "No, ma'am, and we need to keep this line open!"

## 18.

SPIRITS FLAGGED IN the Chevy as Harry and Lucie closed the flat miles of cornfields that separated them from Indianapolis. They had no radio. It was frustrating to be part of something momentous and not be privy to the reaction.

"So what's the wedding ring for, Harry?" Lucie asked. "Disguise?"

"Looking at a married man, Lucie. Since six weeks ago. Don't worry, she's visiting her mother."

It was barely 3:00 o'clock when, circling the Soldiers and Sailors Monument in the heart of town and finding North Meridian Street, Harry ordered, "Now scrunch *way* down."

The coupé nudged into a neighborhood of big old houses— *Rooms to Let* signs in various stages of decay in their windows—mixed with two-story apartment houses. They drove up an alley behind a U-shaped, Spanish-style apartment house with a band of tiles below broad eaves, and turned into an old stable converted to a garage.

"All right, just act normal," said Harry, taking her arm as she got out of the car. "Don't give anybody reason to remember you."

"I'll try."

"Just do it."

They entered the building through a back door, meeting nobody, climbed to the second floor and went down the hall. The floor was terra-cotta tile, the walls a frothy plaster. They heard footsteps. Harry unlocked a door, pushed Lucie inside and listened as the steps faded away.

She surveyed the place. It wasn't much. They stood in the living room. A Pullman kitchen opened to one side; off the other was a small bedroom and smaller bathroom.

"Well—" said Lucie. "For a day or two."

"Glad you approve," said Harry. He locked the door, switched on the radio and poured himself a drink. Lucie accepted one, too, and plopped herself into a chair.

The Mills Brothers were singing *Lulu's Back in Town* when, as if on cue, a flurried announcer cut in with, "We have a WKBF News Flash! Heiress Lucie Spode White of Falls City was kidnapped this morning from her husband's mansion! Latest reports say the gang that did the job vanished heading south! Whether the kidnappers have demanded ransom is not yet known! That's a WKBF News Flash!"

The Mills Brothers resumed their harmonies.

The news perked them up. Smiling beatifically, Harry toasted her.

"You're famous, Lucie."

"Didn't I say this would be fun?" she said. "So the wife's away?"

"Just across town, but we have the night."

"Well, Harry, I'm impressed that you did it. Not a bad start. Carry it off and we'll be fine."

"Bet on it," Harry murmured, all dimples and teeth. Taking the arm of her chair, he buried his face in her hair.

"I'll just freshen up," she said.

When she came out of the bathroom, she sat down on the edge of the bed and took off shoes and stockings and dress. He began yanking off his clothes.

She snapped open her purse.

"Nuh-*uh*," Harry said. "Not this time."

Lucie shrank back, for the first time afraid.

"Harry, I never —"

"Always a first time," he said.

"But Harry, I *can't* —"

"You'll love it," he said, and kissed her. Her mouth refused him, and he shoved her back on the bed and after a struggle forced her legs apart. She fought like a wildcat, and both were panting when he prevailed. This animal intrusion was new in Lucie's experience — dirty and loathsome.

They weren't quiet. Besides her cries of resistance and Harry's groans of pleasure, there was the frantic obbligato of bedsprings. But the racket elicited only a neighbor's weary knocking on the wall.

When Harry finished, Lucie brought up her legs and grabbed her belly, rolling in pain and tears. She felt slimed, intimately slimed. Her whole being revolted.

Harry lit a cigarette.

"C'mon, honey, got to get in there."

"In where?"

"There."

Still crying, she pulled on her dress and, with no idea what was happening, was guided by Harry's one-handed grip on her shoulder to the open closet door.

It was a bedroom closet, nothing more, empty but for a blanket, wooden pail and roll of toilet paper.

He tried to push her inside. Rebelling, she let the force of his hand bend her at the waist.

"Come on, Harry, what's this about?"

"It's for your protection."

"*Protection?*"

"Catch us cozying up, you won't get your money, but you *will* get in trouble with your husband, maybe even the law."

"The *law?*"

"Attempted extortion?"

"But Harry, I don't want to—"

"Don't expect *me* to go down for *you*, sister." He pushed at her hips and she tumbled into the far wall—four feet away—and onto the dusty floorboards. She heard the key turn.

"Harry," she called.

"No talking now, Lucie."

"Harry, I'm hungry."

"Be quiet and wait."

"Harry?"

No answer.


# 19.

JOE DASHED BACK to town and teletyped Washington the ransom note's text—the Bureau preferred teletype as being instantaneous and secure—and asked authorization to telephone the intermediary it named. The teletype's print head chattered back and forth typing his message, then rested.

Bells ringing, it clattered back to life, jerking paper into the bin with the answer.

He ripped it off the wire. It granted him permission, and informed him that a team of agents was en route by train and also told him to phone the Director that evening.

Joe used his siren getting back out to Overridge. At its gates he was directed next door to the gates of Indianola Farm.

Amidst the only slightly lesser throng there, a rifleman admitted him and he drove up to the daunting columns of the house. Indianola's mansion was a specimen of what Tara came to exemplify a few years later, but considerably bigger than the movie manse, larger even than Overridge.

He rang. After a long minute, the door swung inward to bring him, to his surprise, face to face with someone he'd never seen before but felt he recognized.

"Why—who are *you?*" he asked.

"I'm Lily Willis." She looked as startled as he felt, but found a ready smile. "Who are *you?*"

"I'm Joe," he said simply.

They gazed at each other.

"Joe. Oh, I'm not the usual door-answerer, but things are in a tizzy."

"I know. I'm from the F.B.I., by the way."

"Then you'll want to come in. I'm old Mr. Spode's nurse."

"Me, too," Joe unaccountably replied. "I mean for the younger Mr. Spode. I mean—"

She shut the door and they stood in the hall sharing a giddy, "*So what do we do now?*" Then some aura of concern spilled down the hallway and snapped the spell—the spell, but not the bond.

"They're in the library," Miss Willis said. "I'll take your hat."

"Albright!" Spode called.

Joe went in. The library was a stately room nearly bereft of books, its walls hung with portraits of men and horses. Chief Eckerdt stood at a window, and plainclothes detectives and uniformed cops milled about.

In front of a blazing fire, the Old Man was heaped in his Bath chair keening his granddaughter's loss. Father and son had a formal tie; Lucie was his own true heir. She shared his essence, that appetite that seeks to satisfy itself without other consideration. Miss Willis sought to calm him, but he began to swivel his head between her and Joe.

Joe reported to Spode, "Sir, the Director authorizes our calling the intermediary."

"Fine," said Spode.

They discussed who was to speak and what was to be said, and Spode sat down at the desk and, after Joe fitted an adjunct earpiece to the receiver, pulled the telephone close. Ringing up the Long Distance operator, he asked for Mr. Vergil Thrall in Memphis, Tennessee. Standing or sitting or crouching, everybody listened breathlessly as the call went through.

"Hello!" shouted Spode. _"Hello!"_

"Hello!" shouted a voice on the other end. _"Hello!"_

"Is this Vergil Thrall?"

"Yes, sir, this is Mr. Thrall. Who's _this?_"

"Vergil, it's Bob Spode."

_"Yes,_ my friend! What a surprise! What can I do for you, sir?"

"It's a serious situation, Verg. My daughter's been kidnapped."

_"No!_ What's that? _Kidnapped?"_

Astonishment leapt over the wire.

"You haven't heard the radio?"

"No, Bob, I haven't," said Thrall. "Just got home from work. Is there anything I can do?"

"Yes, Verg, there is. I need—_we_ need—a go-between to facilitate paying ransom to free my girl."

Thrall hesitated.

"Bob, of course I'll do anything I can to help. But isn't that a job for the police, or the Federal authorities?"

"The ransom note specifically instructs me not to contact them."

"All right, Bob, but still — my advice would be that you *do*. What prompted you to think of calling *me?*"

"The ransom note again. It asks for $100,000 and — " Spode broke off, confused by Joe's sudden windmilling.

Joe gave a gesture of giving up. Too late now to withhold the amount asked for.

"Bob, I don't follow."

"It names *you*, Verg: 'My intermediary,' it says, 'Vergil Thrall of Memphis, Tennessee.'"

"Good God!" said Thrall. The shock seemed sincere. Joe closed his eyes to listen better. "Well, Bob, I'm shocked and surprised at *that*. *My* name's in the *ransom* note?"

"Well, Verg, you know we have to wonder if maybe Harry's mixed up in this?"

There was a pause.

"I — I hope not, Bob. Sincerely. As I say, I'm shocked. No, Harry couldn't be part of this. There's no harm in the boy, whatever else there may be."

Joe signaled, trying to get a question across. Spode nodded and asked, "Where *is* your son, Verg?"

Joe gave him a thumbs up.

"Don't know if I can rightly tell you, Bob. I mean, would if I could, but he married a young lady just a few weeks ago. Honeymooned at Niagara Falls, but where they've set up housekeeping I don't know. Haven't heard from him in a while. We're hoping it will settle him, particularly after his failure up in Falls City."

"I see. I see. Well, Verg, I guess from this end that's all there is for now. Please take down my number." Spode dictated it: Falls City 1.

"Good luck to you, Bob, and to the young lady's mother and husband, too. I'll do anything I can. Guess I can only wait to hear — ?"

Making his decision, Joe took the receiver out of Spode's hand.

"Mr. Thrall? Sir, this is Special Agent Joseph Albright, Federal Bureau of Investigation."

"Who? Yes? F.B.I.?" Thrall momentarily sounded infirm at everything implicit in the young man's interruption.

"Mr. Thrall, the Bureau is on the case already, but please keep that to yourself. We'll not hinder you in any way from complying with whatever the kidnappers want you to do," Joe told him. "But you must keep us informed of whatever they ask. Do you follow me, sir?"

"You're not sending men?"

"To Memphis? No, sir, aside from myself: Soon as the ransom can be gotten together, I'll bring it down and hand it over personally. The Bureau's priority is the same as the family's: All we want is their little girl home safe and sound."

"I think I see, sir," said Mr. Thrall. "You have my business address, Thrall & Hawkins Constructors, Harmonia Building, Memphis?"

"Yes, sir." Already Thrall's house and office were being watched and the telephones tapped, but Joe didn't tell him that. He offered only, "And we'll need photographs of your son."

"Of course."

"Thank you, sir."

Joe hung up and turned to Spode.

"Well, he's not in on it," he said.

"My impression also," said Spode. "But that son —!"

"One pressing point, sir: The banks open at 9:00 in the morning, but to get together so large a sum — *if* you intend to pay it — I suggest we notify the Treasury and —"

"Intend to, and will," Spode interrupted, and walked up to the largest picture on the wall.

It was an imaginary portrait of his great-great-grandfather, the first Spode to settle the Qwattata Valley, within a garish gilded frame. His own father had posed for its painter, Harvey Joiner, 30 years earlier. The pioneer in the picture, garbed in leather and the fur of bear and fox, their textures contrasting with the shiny steel rifle and axe in his hands, looked like an All-American variation on a wily Renaissance pope.

Spode swung the portrait out from the wall, revealing the door of a safe. Twirling its dial with practiced precision, he clicked it open and began removing wrapped stacks of $20 bills and stuffing them into a Gladstone bag. He counted them, replaced several, counted again, closed the safe, twirled the dial, pushed the portrait back to the wall and presented the bag to Joe Albright.

"A hundred thousand dollars? There you go."

## 20.

VERGIL THRALL HUNG UP the phone and poured himself a drink. He was a compact, distinguished-looking man in his mid-50s, already white haired, if with a face youthfully unlined and mobile. But there were distinct furrows across his forehead as he chipped at the ice.

Home from work early—the Depression helped him keep banker's hours—he'd walked through the door and heard the telephone ringing. It was a beautiful afternoon in Memphis, with a hint of seasonal coolness. The Thrall house stood in a gracious eastern suburb, a big stucco Colonial whose particular feature was the series of terraces and gardens in back.

Thrall saw his wife on one of the terraces, as yet unaware

that he was home, much less that a conversation with the F.B.I. had just changed their lives. She gripped her clippers as though only the prospect of a plant needing pruning could justify lingering in the beautiful light.

He thought he wouldn't share the news with her. Not immediately.

First he tore a page out of his address book. It had an Indianapolis entry for his son and new daughter-in-law.

He burned the page in an ashtray.

On second thought, he burned the whole book in the fireplace, and crushed the ash to crumbs.

Then, with regret but no hesitation, he went into his wife's sewing room, found her address book and burned it, too. Also he rifled a drawer, found two letters from their son postmarked Indianapolis and burned them.

She was a good woman, good wife, good mother. He hoped he was a good man, good husband, good father. But what is the judgment when the son is rotten?

Thrall fell heavily into his chair and shook his glass so the ice chinked.

He loved his son. Loved his rotten only child; undoubtedly always would, come what may. It was amusing and appalling to watch him grow up coasting on the charm he was born with, lazy from the age of diapers, aimless and harmless as Huckleberry Finn until the fatal age of 12, when he discovered girls. That was it. That was the ballgame.

After a prematurely harrowing high-school career, Harry attended Vanderbilt Law (then an undergraduate school), but inevitably got a girl pregnant. The boy was incorrigible. Hence shipping him up to Falls City.

And when that didn't work, his pants on fire brought him to what his father thought a just fate in the person of Mabel, older and cagier. Mabel told Harry she was carrying his child and expected him to marry her. He did it, too—this one would brook no refusal. His parents attended the City Hall ceremony. A great relief, as was the nuptial couple's removal to Mabel's hometown of Indianapolis, shortly before she informed Harry she had miscarried.

But his son a *kidnapper?*

A kidnapper, yet, who would put his own father's name in a ransom note?

No, *that* rang true. That was pure Harry. The young idiot could well be behind this mess.

Sipping his bourbon, Thrall reluctantly assessed his own legal position.

Not his fault he was named intermediary. No liability there, surely. But if Harry asked him to *do* something and he *did* it, he would be culpable—guilty of Federal crime. Unless, he supposed, he informed on his son, as the Feds had asked, and they were to tell him to do as Harry wanted.

By the same token, although the F.B.I. could order him around to its heart's content, his obligation was a father's. If Harry were committing a capital offense—as the new Lindbergh Law classed kidnapping—what father outside of one in the Bible would help send his son to the Chair?

Sighing against the dusk gathering in the room, he walked outdoors.

He found his wife greedily snipping chrysanthemums. She turned at his step, their mellow reflection gilding her face.

He squeezed and kissed her, and coyly she said, "Why, Vergil Thrall, you old devil! What's got into you?"

He lacked the words to say.

"I am so tired, Marian. Going to bed early."

"What's wrong?"

"Just tired," he said. "Rotten tired."

## 21.

JOE DECLINED SPODE'S offer of dinner, even when Miss Willis spontaneously began to second the invitation (until the Old Man's sudden choking claimed her attention). He had a private telephone call to make. Driving back to his office, he called a number in Washington, D.C.

"OK, Albright, what've we got?" asked J. Edgar Hoover.

Joe briefed him, and summed up: "It's a confusing situation, sir. That the note names a past associate of Mr. Spode's as intermediary, and that Spode employed this man's son earlier this year, might suggest—"

"He know the girl?" Hoover barked.

"I'm guessing the maid thinks so. Says different, but my guess is they knew each other pretty well. She quotes her saying, 'Hurry, let's go.'"

"*Shit,*" said Hoover. The gaudy ramifications pulsed over the line. "*Shit,* a pseudo-kidnapping?" He pronounced his fancy word *swaydo.* "Won't do, Joe. This sort of thing gets people excited. If the *millionaires* aren't safe in this country, who *is?* And if the millionaires are *conning* each other—well, might as well go Bolshevik right now! Have to find that son of a bitch and nail him to the wall!"

"I think I hear what you're saying, sir."

"Best thing for her and the family—for all of us, whatever the facts—is get this guy and put him away. Save that poor girl—from herself, if necessary. That's our job."

"Yes, sir."

"Get my teletype? Two men coming by the 9:30 train?"

"Thank you, sir."

"And I'm sending Special Agent Sturgis on my plane in the morning." He meant the F.B.I.'s famous ace Melvin Sturgis, who personally executed Dillinger and Pretty Boy Floyd with shots to the head. "Pick him up at Spode Field around 9:00 a.m."

"Oh please God not Melvin," said Joe, then thought: *Jesus, did I say that out loud?*

Hoover heard him, but let it pass. He knew Melvin Sturgis to be the Bureau's Showboater Number One, but as a matter of politics and budget, that showboater was useful to him.

"He'll run things at the house," Hoover assured him. "You get the ransom to Memphis safe and sound."

"Yes, sir!"


# 22.


AFTER HARRY HAD a nap, curiosity got the better of him. As darkness fell he decided to go out for the evening papers.

First he had to tie up Lucie.

He opened the closet door. She flinched at the sudden light, scrabbled to the wall and cowered, arms over her head.

"C'mon, Lucie, don't be like that. *Sheesh*, makes me feel bad. Look, I need to tie you up." When she didn't respond he said, "*Hello?* Remember me?"

"Not tying me up," she muttered.

"Going out. Cops bust in and find you sitting around la-di-dah? Think about it."

She glared.

"Look, Lucie, this might not be *nice,* but just think how *nice* 50,000 bucks is."

"Can I use the bathroom first?"

"Hurry up."

On her return—the bathroom window still painted shut, still too small for her to get through—she submitted. Harry tied her arms behind her back, and she sat on the floor.

"Too tight," she complained. "And I'm hungry."

"I'll bring something back."

He taped her mouth shut with adhesive tape and locked the closet door.

When he returned with the papers, he ripped the tape off. She sputtered for breath while he untied her hands.

"I need the bathroom again."

"Nothing doing. You got a bucket, *use* it."

He tossed her a ham sandwich and locked the door, quick.

Keeping an ear open, he settled down in the living room with the Indianapolis *Star* and Chicago *Daily News*. The headlines were huge, but the news scanty:

# SPODE HEIRESS
# KIDNAPPED
## *DARING GANG INVADES*
## *MANSION BEDROOM!*

The stories were about reporters covering other reporters. They gave ample descriptions of newsreel cameramen thronging the gates of Overridge, of newsmen searching the riverside and accompanying the Coast Guard as it probed Four Mile Island and Persimmon Point.

Both papers ran the same photograph of the victim dressed

for an evening out, jewels sparkling and eyes glassy, and laid out the selflessness of her life, from her good works with the Junior League to her flower arrangements for the annual Bandits Bacchanal.

There was also a heart-tugging picture taken that day by an enterprising photographer who vaulted Indianola Farm's fence at first word of the abduction. It showed the snatched heiress's legendary grandfather in his Bath chair clinging to his nurse.

What delighted Harry was the fear and respect with which they spoke of the "brutal kidnapping gang."

Got *that* right, he thought.

## 23.

JOE ALBRIGHT MET the train from Chicago at the FC&A Station that evening.

Two colleagues got off — David and Casey, friends from his training course. The three young men, dressed in gray suits, gray fedoras, and with similar subtle hitches to their walks from the weight of the guns on their left sides, fell into step down the platform. People hung back at the sight, as though big-city gangsters were come to town at last.

They were at Indianola Farm by 10:00 o'clock, where their night was just beginning. After showing them the scene of the crime next door, Joe took over the dining room table, a lake of polished mahogany that could accommodate 26. He dropped Spode's Gladstone bag on it, locked the double doors, blocked the swinging door to the butler's pantry, divided the cash hoard into three piles and distributed pads, pencils and fountain pens.

"Two things we have to do to each bill," Joe said. "First, record the serial number—and we lucked out, these are wrapped bills, numbers are sequential. Kidnapper didn't say otherwise, so they should be good. Next, mark 'em. Any ideas?"

"Two blue dots on Andy Jackson's cheek?" Casey suggested.

"How 'bout *one* blue dot?" asked David.

"Fine," Joe said.

"Hundred G in twenties—5,000 bills to mark?" David complained. "Jesus, take all night."

"Sooner we get started," Joe answered. "I'll keep the coffee coming."

But Miss Willis undertook that task. She brought in the first fresh-brewed cups a few minutes later. While she was setting them out, exchanging a comfortable, confidential smile with Joe, there arose in the background a weird, high-pitched sound that Joe belatedly realized came from the Old Man, throwing a tantrum worthy of a two-year-old. Blanching, Miss Willis ran out of the room.

It was a long night's work. Recording the numbers was the easy part. They noted those of the top bills in all 50 straps, and that gave them the range for each. It took longer to tattoo Old Hickory.

Joe opened the windows so the breeze off the river could refresh the room. Once or twice the faces of watchmen tramping the grounds caught the light as they peered curiously indoors. As dawn approached an army of birds also went on watch.

Joe was elated when they finished. Sleepiness fought elation, until Miss Willis materialized at his side with a cup of coffee, when elation won out.

"Thank you, Miss Willis," he said in tones so warm his colleagues sniggered.

## 24.

LUCIE WAITED TO USE the bucket until she could hear Harry breathing softly, asleep. Afterwards, sitting on the floor amidst the smell of her body wastes, she was nauseous.

She tried to think of what to do. But she was shorn of options. The door was locked — she stealthily turned the knob both ways and pushed: *Locked*. She didn't have the key, nor anything she could employ as a key, save for the bobbie pins in her hair.

Taking one, she pushed it into the keyhole, but nothing caught or engaged, tumbled or unlocked. She tried using two, with the same lack of result. The faint scratching seemed to incite restlessness in the bed, so she ceased.

There was no other door. No window. No opening of any kind. The ceiling intrigued her — might there be an attic hatch? Doubtful, but she had to know. But, standing up, she couldn't reach it, and walking up the walls was nothing she could undertake without noise. She tried, but accidentally knocked against the floor and heard a sleepy murmur from the bed.

Anyway, Harry was right: Escaping would make the whole thing a waste. Stick it out and she'd reap her reward — *if* she could trust Harry.

Meanwhile, exhausted as she was, she refused to sleep on a closet floor.

Hours later her body seized awake on the planking. A

shard of daylight showed beneath the door. Pressing her eye to the crack, she saw what looked like the edge of a rug.

A woman was in the apartment—a woman whose penetrating voice had awakened her. It came nearer, insisting, "Show her to me, Harry. I want to see her."

"No, Mabel, best you never lay eyes on her."

"Just one glance. They say she's pretty."

"Not as pretty as you, Doll Face."

But there came a knocking on the closet door.

"Mrs. White?" asked the same strident voice. "Are you hungry?"

"Yes," Lucie ventured, after a pause.

"I'm going to open the door and put in a plate and spoon," said the woman. "Harry's right here and he has a gun, so don't you move."

The key turned. When the door opened Lucie had her face poised to catch whatever the light might disclose about the ceiling.

It disclosed only smooth plaster and the undersides of shelves.

She looked at Mabel, who looked back in mixed disdain and triumph. Mabel, never a handsome woman, clearly had half a dozen years on Harry.

"Here you go, dear," she said brightly. "No one ever called me a great cook, but Harry managed to choke it down."

Scrambled eggs and bacon, with sliced tomato.

"Thank you," Lucie said after a pause, heaving herself upright and taking the plate.

"You're on the radio, dear," Mabel said. "You're *famous*."

The door closed. Lucie ate a little, but the smell from the bucket interfered and she put the plate on the floor.

Lucie learned nothing more that morning except that Harry and Mabel were not discreet in their lovemaking. Mabel was first loudly coy, then loudly demanding, and there came again the weary knocking on the wall.

## 25.

DAVID DROVE CASEY AND JOE—and the bag of money cuffed to Joe's wrist—out to Spode Field to meet Melvin Sturgis, windows open to help them stay awake. Joe and Casey would fly on to Memphis in the same Bureau plane that was delivering Showboater Number One to Falls City.

They parked beside the new terminal, a streamlined Deco confection that, standing still, appeared to be moving faster than either of the planes that soon buffeted the air from opposite directions. One was the F.B.I.'s Ford Tri-Motor; the smaller craft bore Pearl White home from his timber camp.

Pearl's plane was made to circle the airfield while Sturgis's swooped straight in, danced side to side on its wheels, and taxied up to the terminal. Larger than life—or at any rate, with a head disproportionately big for his body—Melvin Sturgis tripped down the steps and came up to Joe.

"Albright? Sturgis. Met at your initiation." A brief, meaning smile. "No photographers?"

"No sir, I knew you wouldn't want any hoopla."

"Good man," said Sturgis, frowning, "but I've learned to respect the public's right to know. They're my partner in crime detection."

But several newsmen and photographers were staking out the airfield to await Pearl's homecoming, and flashes now went off, with a pacifying effect on Sturgis.

While Pearl's plane touched down and rolled towards where his Cadillac awaited him, Sturgis told Joe, "Wouldn't believe the excitement this little case of yours is causing at headquarters. Biggest thing since Lindbergh. They say the Spodes are rich as hell?"

"Yes, sir."

"Fill me in."

Joe rapidly did so.

"Good, good," Sturgis said. "One thing, Albright: Now that I'm here, we need results. The public expects it, and Eddie—I mean Mr. Hoover—wouldn't send me except on that understanding."

"Sir?"

"Do I make myself clear?"

"Yes, sir," said Joe.

"That the ransom?" Regarding the Gladstone bag chained to Joe's wrist, Sturgis sneered, "Look like a Wall Street messenger boy." To shock him, he added, "Don't go getting any ideas."

"No, *sir!*" said Joe—shocked.

The door of Pearl's plane opened and, grasping a rifle, Pearl jumped to the tarmac. More flashes popped. Sturgis strode through the knot of people waving his hand.

"There goes Hot Dog," Casey murmured.

"Has to get in the picture," said David.

"Mr. White?" Sturgis was calling. "Melvin Sturgis, F.B.I.! We're on the case, sir!"

Switching his rifle to the other hand, Pearl shook Sturgis's. Flashes blossomed and questions were shouted.

"We're taking the situation very seriously," Sturgis announced, showing the oversized teeth in his oversized head. "Everything is proceeding. More than that I'm not at liberty to say." To Pearl, he said, "Sir, we will follow you."

"'Preciate your help," Pearl muttered.

His chauffeur trading the Cadillac's wheel for the rifle, Pearl drove himself home. Sturgis followed, driven by David in Joe's Ford.

Meanwhile Joe and Casey boarded the Ford Tri-Motor, climbed the steeply raked aisle and settled into velvet club chairs across from each other.

One by one the engines started up. The plane moved down the runway, sped up, vibrated alarmingly—and was launched. It climbed to altitude and leveled out, and Joe and Casey watched the green swaddling blanket below, occasionally cleared by farms or towns and in places fraying into autumn splendor. They were too excited to nap.

J. Edgar Hoover's personal steward—a slight young special agent with yellow hair—served Danish and coffee.

# 26.

VERGIL THRALL WOKE UP from a dead sleep knowing what he must do. As for his son, he thought, *What fools ye mortals be.*

He breakfasted with his wife as usual and told her what to say should Harry happen to telephone.

"Is Harry going to call?" she asked, bewildered but hopeful.

"Maybe. If he does, tell him, 'Dad says, "I spy, with my little eye, the pyramids."'"

"Honey, that doesn't make sense. Besides, don't you mean 'something that begins—'"

"Please say it."

"'I spy the *pyramids*'?"

"That's it. Tell him, 'Dad said to say, "I spy the pyramids."'"

"All right, Vergil."

"You have it?"

"Daddy says, 'I spy the pyramids.'"

As always, Thrall took the streetcar to work. It was a straight shot of two miles, ten minutes. He looked discreetly around to see if, despite Joe's pledge, Federal agents were shadowing him. There was one possibility — a dark-suited man he'd never seen before — but he didn't feel inclined to try to flush him out. It was not to his purpose to show himself conscious of being watched or tailed.

Accordingly, he got off at his customary corner and entered the Harmonia Building, as usual stepping to the newsstand off the busy lobby to buy his cigar and newspapers. The Harmonia was the finest office building in Memphis, built by Thrall's firm just before the Crash. The lobby murals of antebellum cotton plantations were painted so vividly the slaves' joyful songs seemed to ring out.

To his relief, Thrall saw no loiterers watching as he stepped across the lobby into the Farmers & Merchants Bank. The manager, Mr. Spielmann, happened to be standing by the door, but Thrall ignored him and walked purposefully towards the manager's brass-fenced desk. Spielmann followed.

"Good morning, Mr. Thrall. What can I do for you?"

"An unusual matter, Mr. Spielmann, and I thought I should first sound you out as to its feasibility. My firm will soon — possibly this morning — be getting in a very great deal of cash."

"Oh yes?" asked Spielmann, interested.

"A hundred thousand dollars, Mr. Spielmann. We would esteem it a great kindness if you could help us exchange these particular bills. It's difficult to explain why —"

"No explanation needed, Mr. Thrall. A hundred thousand,

you say?"

Spielmann's eyes went out of focus to ponder the challenge, even as he bent to open the half-gate in the railing, gestured Thrall into a chair and took his own. It wouldn't be easy, but it could be done, and he was a man who prided himself on customer service.

"Yes, I think we can undertake that," he said. "Have to call some other banks, ask for a little help, is all. Your account will be charged point zero five, of course."

"We're most grateful. And if the bills were to vary in denomination, that also might better suit — "

"Of course, sir, I understand completely. If I might ask, is this in connection with the Cuba project — ?"

Thrall & Hawkins, in casting about for work in Latin America — construction in North America being at a sickening standstill — had turned up a sugar mill in Cuba that wanted their expertise.

"I'm sure I don't know what you mean, Mr. Spielmann," Thrall murmured, smiling. "But it seems that south of the border they do business in a — a different kind of way."

"Friends in high places, eh?" Spielmann winked. "Count on us, sir. Terrible business up there in Falls City, isn't it?"

Startled, Thrall agreed.

"You know the Spodes, I believe?" Spielmann asked.

"Yes, we built the Spode Tower," Thrall said. "Awful thing. I feel for Mr. Spode, as any father would. Fine man. Fine family."

He thanked Spielmann again and took an elevator upstairs, where Thrall & Hawkins occupied the fourth floor, and where a man standing against the wall had a Federal look to him.

Nodding at him, Thrall greeted his receptionist and entered his company's offices.

## 27.

THE DIRECTOR'S PLANE found the broad brown road that is the Mississippi, followed it and swooped in for a landing on the new asphalt runway at Memphis Municipal Airport. A Bureau car was waiting, a black Ford V-8 driven by Bruce, Joe's opposite number in Memphis.

Bruce briefed Joe and Casey on the results of the night's surveillance of Thrall's house. They'd been careful to leave him alone to see what might transpire.

"Nil," he reported. "No visitors, no calls in or out, except for yours, and no one left the house till 9:30 a.m., when Thrall went to work."

"Good," said Joe.

"We're watching his office and tapping the phones, but it's a pretty big outfit."

"Right."

From Bruce's office Joe made a quick call to Indianola Farm to report his arrival to Melvin Sturgis.

Sturgis had some advice for him.

"Stick to Thrall like stink on shit, Albright," he said. "He's the key to this thing. Meanwhile, doing what I can here." He dropped his voice. "That little nurse? Pretty sure she wants to feel my gun."

Bruce drove Joe and Casey the three blocks to the Harmonia Building. Going inside, Joe pulled his coat sleeve low to hide the handcuff linking him to the Gladstone bag. On the fourth floor they collected their colleague leaning against the wall, identified themselves to the receptionist and told her they wished to see Vergil Thrall.

She said as much into an intercom, and Vergil promptly opened the door behind her desk, greeted them and invited them into his office.

They crowded in, four intimidating young men in gray suits, and introduced themselves.

Vergil welcomed them. Suggesting they might be more comfortable in the adjoining conference room, he conducted them through a side door into a long, light-filled room whose windows overlooked old warehouses along the Mississippi. Joe rested the Gladstone bag on the tabletop, delved in his pocket for a key, unlocked the handcuffs and opened the bag.

"Well sir, here's what we brought you," he said, displaying the bricks of cash. "One hundred thousand dollars."

Vergil nodded gravely.

"Very good, sir. I appreciate it."

As Thrall signed the Bureau's receipt, Joe rubbed his raw wrist and asked, "Now, if you'll tell us what the kidnapper has instructed you to do?"

"I've received no instructions of any sort, sir. No one's yet been in contact with me." Vergil frowned at the bag, reached over and snapped it shut. "Will you permit me to put this money in my safe? It makes me nervous."

"Certainly, sir."

"Oh, and you wanted a photograph of Harry," Vergil said, bringing out a small snapshot dating to his son's sophomore year in high school.

Joe took it and, while he studied it, his fellows crowding around, Vergil casually hauled the Gladstone bag into his office. After issuing orders about making and distributing enlarged photostatic copies of the photo, Joe turned the knob of the office door.

To his surprise, it was locked.

He knocked, saying confidentially, "Mr. Thrall? Mr. Thrall?" He knocked louder, raising his voice: "Mr. Thrall, open up, please, sir. . . You have to open the door, sir. . . *Now*."

Casey, Bruce and Tommy dashed towards the conference room's other door, and to their consternation found it locked also. They rattled it, and at the end of a long minute it was opened by the draughtsman their noise disturbed across the hall. He blinked resentfully.

"Where'd he go?" Casey asked.

"Who?"

"Vergil Thrall."

"Don't know, sir."

They ran out and around to the receptionist and found the door there to Vergil's office also locked. Together they summarily broke it open, and entered with guns drawn.

The office was empty.

Breaking into the conference room, they let Joe in. There was no safe that any of them could find.

The receptionist confirmed the obvious, that Thrall had left.

"OK," barked Joe. "*Find* him."

They split up, each taking a different corridor. Joe stole down the central passage. Rooms on one side held draughtsmen, while clerks worked on the other.

Joe checked every office, every closet, every storeroom, while in his head, gremlin versions of J. Edgar Hoover and Melvin Sturgis began to berate his wits and competence, and to mock his prospects with the Bureau.

## 28.

VERGIL THRALL GRABBED the Gladstone bag and walked rapidly through his office — the door locking behind him — and, a finger to his lips, past his receptionist to the staircase next to the elevators.

In six fast-charging bouts he was downstairs. He sidled along the wall to Farmers & Merchants — no one appeared to be watching for him — and found Spielmann attending his desk like a vestal, rubbing his hands together, pleased with himself and eyeing Vergil's Gladstone bag with delight. A stocky young guard and two clerks stood by.

"Ah, perfect timing, Mr. Thrall. I must say, I'm amazed how fast we were able to do this. First National was *most* helpful."

The cash, ready to go, lay in a canvas sack on his desk.

"Good man, Mr. Spielmann," Vergil said.

"Thank you, sir."

His clerks dug into Vergil's bag, scooping out Spode's re-wrapped bundles. They riffled the edges expertly, as though they could hear the count, jotted down amounts, compared them and declared themselves satisfied.

After having Vergil sign a receipt, Spielmann dumped the canvas sack's contents into the empty Gladstone bag, making it bulkier and heavier than before, though still manageable. Vergil declined his invitation to count it.

"Mr. Spielmann, can't tell you how grateful the firm is."

"Happy to be of service, Mr. Thrall. Do you wish a guard to accompany you upstairs?"

"Thank you, that won't be necessary."

Pulling his hat low, Vergil left the bank, went along the lobby wall to the rear exit and out, moments before Joe burst into the lobby.

On the second floor of the adjoining garage Vergil

approached a Thrall & Hawkins company car. Though to the eye no different from any other brown Ford V-8, it was specially sprung to withstand jouncing over construction sites. Having provided himself with its key upstairs, he unlocked it, got in, stashed the money on the floor, started the motor and drove down a ramp and onto Broadway.

Joe was running towards the same ramp, after making a spectacle of himself sweeping the lobby, darting into bank and newsstand, then blundering through the back door into the garage. He arrived on the sidewalk just in time to see the brown Ford vanish through an intersection. He couldn't be certain Vergil was driving, but instinct told him he was, and further instructed him to try the door of the Bureau Ford parked at the curb in hopes it was unlocked.

It was.

Joe jumped in, roared the powerful engine to life and made a dizzying U-turn as his colleague Bruce ran out of the Harmonia Building.

Joe paused to yell from across the street, "Chasing Thrall! I'll call in!"

And he was gone, speeding up Broadway and beseeching instinct to tell him which way to turn.

CROSSING THE RIVER, Vergil took U.S. 61 north. It would carry him as far as Minneapolis, unless he first turned off for someplace like St. Louis or Chicago or, 150 miles away, Cairo, Illinois.

It was a sunny, beautiful fall day and, as best he could make out, no one was following him. But he dared not relax and enjoy the drive. The stakes were too high. Too much could go wrong. Too many elements were out of his control. He could be chased and caught. He might encounter roadblocks, or a sudden thunderstorm might wash out the road—it was prone to that.

And what if Harry didn't call?

What if he called, but his mother forgot to say "I spy the pyramids"?

What if he called and she said it, but Harry didn't get it?

## 29.

HARRY INSISTED THAT Mabel follow routine, so she went to her job selling costume jewelry at the big Monument Circle Woolworth's. Also following routine, Harry lounged around the apartment all morning.

To Harry, his scheme's final touch was naming his father as go-between. He had full confidence in his Dad's loyalty — and ingenuity. Meanwhile *he* could rest, keep up with the news, guard Lucie — and wait. When it came time for him to do something, his intermediary would let him know.

Though he also thought that he might just give the old Dad a call — a quick call, from a public phone.

He was, he realized, too tense, too restless.

He needed to relax if he was not to start making mistakes.

Lucie heard him enter the bedroom and come up to the closet. His shadow for a moment extinguishing her thin line of daylight along the door's bottom, she died a little death.

He unlocked the door and yanked her onto the bed.

"God, you need a bath," he announced. "You *stink*."

She lay back, smoothing her smart gray dress, determined to talk fast, talk him out of another naked insertion, even as Harry pulled down his pants, opened his shirt, came up astride her and presented the awful thing to her lips.

"No!" she said, turning her head. "Harry, my family will pay *anything* — "

"Already in gear, Lucie. Shut up and turn this way."

"No, really, let me go now, I promise they'll *double* — "

With both hands he wrenched her head around.

"Harry, you can keep it *all,* if — Harry, no, no, I'll *die*, don't kill me, *please* don't kill me."

"Wouldn't ever kill *you*, baby," he assured her as he stuffed her mouth. "Worth too much alive. Oh baby, *knew* you could do it."

She drowned, actually drowned until she figured out how to breathe through her nose.

"Please — cover — those — *teeth*," Harry urged.

She gagged again and again.

"Yeah, baby, yeah, like *that*," he said, and with a grunt slimed her mouth and, after a long suspense — for her, of pure nausea — withdrew. She curled up gagging, choking and crying.

"You're *good*, Lucie," he told her. "Best in every department."

Without resistance he tied her hands behind her back, taped her mouth and pushed her back into the closet.

He left her alone with her beating heart. She couldn't fathom or absorb what had just happened. She had an awful taste in her mouth, wanted to retch, but with her mouth taped shut had to suppress the impulse. *Had* to.

And in her deepest parts she felt germs of slime from the day before penetrating her womb. She was sure of it.

## 30.

HARRY FELT A LOT BETTER.

Confident Lucie was subdued, he strolled downtown. Thought he'd make that call. At random he chose a drugstore with a Public Telephone sign, folded the booth's door closed and, through the Operator, made a collect call to his father's house, giving the name of an uncle.

It went through almost instantly. Harry assumed the F.B.I. would be listening in and trying to trace it. He thought he knew from the movies (such was the quality of his research) that it would take a call lasting several minutes for them to do so. Tracing it to a pay phone a mile from where he had Lucie wouldn't solve the crime for them, but as he didn't want them to know so much as the state where she was — especially when the newspapers still unaccountably spoke of a flight south — he intended to hang up shy of the one-minute mark.

He'd know in that minute if his father were home. He'd know something.

Harry kept his eyes on his watch's sweep hand as he listened to his mother accept the charges.

"*Ma?*"

"Harry! Your father *said* you might call. How *are* — ?"

"Ma, put Dad on the line."

"He's at the office. Is anything the matter? Harry, can't you tell me if — ?"

"Ma, I'm *fine*. But I don't have any *time*."

Something prompted her. She blurted, "Dad said to tell you, 'I spy the pyramids.' 'With my little eye — '"

Harry hung up as though his fingers burned. His watch told him 17 seconds had elapsed. Safe! They might have heard him, but nothing that would do them any good.

Except "I spy the pyramids"?

But Harry, picking up the pace, realized that *he* knew what his Dad meant, and the F.B.I. wouldn't. No chance!

Brilliant!

Brilliant old Daddy!

They'd heard it, could *almost* figure it out. "I spy the pyramids." Anyone could realize it referred to one of those games people play to pass the time traveling, could unfold a map and pore over it. Nashville has its Parthenon, Birmingham its Vulcan. But only Cairo boasts the Pyramids. Cairo, Egypt, that is; Cairo, Illinois is the flat wedge of land where the Ohio River pays tribute to the Mississippi, a town whose riverboat prosperity sailed away long ago.

Harry laughed out loud at his father's misdirection — laughed so hard an approaching mother swerved her toddler towards a storefront's protection.

Because Cairo, Illinois wasn't quite it either. The police might converge there, but he'd be meeting up with his intermediary — and collecting the ransom — someplace else. And now he knew exactly where.

But enough. There was work to be done.

He dropped into Woolworth's and whispered to Mabel that he'd be gone 24 hours or so, but then they'd be done. Could she handle Lucie by herself in the meantime?

"That scared cow?"

"Well then, come on."

Her manager yelled after her — it was lunchtime, they were busy — but Mabel had just retired.

Once home Harry had a qualm about leaving his hostage with her, but Mabel reassured him.

"When I was a little girl, a mouse got in my closet?" she said. "I stuffed newspaper under the door. He nibbled and nibbled, slower and slower. After a few days I opened the door and there he was, *dead.* So don't worry about Lucie. Won't get to *me.*"

"OK, but we don't want her dead, either. She's the golden goose, remember."

Harry filled a Thermos with coffee, Mabel made sandwiches, and he left. After gassing up the Chevy coupé and checking the tires, he found U.S. 40, the old National Road. It took him west out of town, soon becoming a two-lane track straight through the harvest fields.

It was a pleasant day for a long drive. At Terre Haute he turned south on U.S. 41, glad to have the sun out of his eyes, intending to cross the Ohio River at Evansville around sunset and then push westward on U.S. 60.

He went on, having a ball.

Two topics held his thoughts.

The first was his appearance. Find a country doctor and get plastic surgery by force, like in the movies? No: Harry had no intention of fooling with his face. He liked his face, and knew he could alter it enough through changes in grooming and expression.

In fact, he took out his comb. Like many vain men, Harry parted his hair on the right side. Now, for the sake of disguise, he pushed his comb the other way. Further, he decided to start a mustache—a nice Ronald Colman mustache—and wear sunglasses like a Hollywood star.

The second topic, even more absorbing, was trying to decide what kind of car to buy with the loot. He lusted after a Duesenberg, but some dim instinct warned that something less flashy might be a better idea. A Buick? Could he go so far as to buy a Buick?

Certainly something with one of those newfangled car radios. That drive up from Falls City the other day? Not to mention today? *Torture,* not having one.

## 31.

JOE KEPT CHASING up the Mississippi, certain — though he couldn't have said why — he was on the right track, but fretful when he didn't overtake Vergil.

But the older man was driving to beat the devil. Carrying precisely the burden of worry and tension his son declined to bear, Vergil locked his hands on the wheel and steered up the road going as fast as he dared, tires barely keeping traction on the pavement, passing trucks, cars and tractors, and averaging fully 40 m.p.h.

Just past New Madrid, Missouri, he turned east off the highway and raced 12 miles along a little road towards the ferry opposite Columbus, Kentucky.

A steep ramp took him to the top of the levee over the Mississippi River. A mile across the water, a wilderness of forest was broken by two blocks of riverside storefronts, giving the mighty Father of Waters a local, little aspect. The river was empty save for a tugboat keeping a barge steady in the middle of the current.

Seeing him, the tug heeled around and pushed the barge to the wharf at the levee. Directed by a teenaged kid, Vergil drove onto it. It was roomy enough for several cars. The kid collected $1 for the toll.

Turning around as the kid chocked his tires, Vergil saw another car coming, and fast!

Heart in mouth, seeing that the captain had spotted the car and was waiting for it, Vergil brought out a $10 bill. The astonished kid took it, waved it at the bridge, and they embarked, the boat pushing the barge across the river. They weren't 50 yards along when a Ford V-8 appeared atop the levee. A young man—Joe Albright—lunged out of it and jumped and yelled and waved his arms like a wild man.

Breathing deep of the river's rich smell, feeling that strong sense of division that crossing the Mississippi always carries, Vergil watched Joe recede.

Joe blew his horn: *NOOOO!* After a minute its tone dropped as if in acceptance, but still it protested: *NOO-OOOO!*

The sound traveled tinnily across the great river in the boat's wake.

BACKTRACKING TO a country store, Joe used its telephone to call Indianola Farm.

Melvin Sturgis reamed him out.

"Get back to Memphis, Albright: A marked bill's been passed already. *That's* where the kidnapper is—probably Mrs. White, too—and *that's* where you belong."

"Look, Mr. Sturgis, Thrall took off like a bat out of hell—I *think* it's Thrall, but hell, I'm chasing *someone*. He's in a brown Ford V-8, and he knows I'm on his tail."

"Could be Thrall, all right," Sturgis remarked without much interest. "Auto of that description belonging to Thrall & Hawkins is missing."

"It's just now crossing the Mississippi! At Columbus, Kentucky!"

"So what, Albright? Action on this one's in Memphis. Oh, and we got an intercept from the phone at Thrall's house. The son calls his mother, she tells him his father says to say, 'I spy the pyramids.' Make anything of it?"

"Exactly!" Joe cried, galvanized. "Cairo, Illinois—*Cairo*, get it? *Pyramids?* It's just up the road!"

"Told you, *Memphis* is where things're busting loose. Hey, there's a Memphis in Egypt, too. Went to college myself, you know."

"*You* going to Memphis?"

"What, leave my little nursie when she wants to play doctor? But *you're* going."

"No, I'm not."

"Your career." Joe could hear his shrug through the wire. "Here, keeping an open line to Washington, Director wanted me to patch you in. Hang on."

It took a minute for Sturgis to fill in the Director on what Joe had told him, but the next voice Joe heard was fussy and abrupt: J. Edgar Hoover's.

"Albright, Sturgis tell you about the tap from Vergil Thrall's house?"

"Yes, sir."

"What do you make of it?" Hoover snapped. "*'I spy the fucking pyramids.'*"

"Means Cairo, Illinois, sir. I know Special Agent Sturgis disagrees, but it's obvious it's Cairo."

"If it's so goddam *obvious* – " Hoover started, but stopped in frustration. "OK, Albright, get up there. I'll have the State Police seal off the place."

"Thanks."

And Hoover was done – slammed down the phone.

*Well, I survived that,* Joe thought. *Surprisingly.*

And rushed back to the levee, and was waiting when the tug pushed its empty barge to the wharf for him.


THINGS IN MEMPHIS were moving fast!

Bruce rushed to the hardware store whose alert cashier compared a bill she took in to the mimeographed list of serial numbers the police brought by.

"Half an hour ago," she told Bruce. "Shifty-eyed gent, needed a plunger—he *says*. Pays with a $20 bill. I looks close and the number checks out, and I says to myself, '*Why*—'"

A runner dispatched by his office tugged at Bruce's coat with news that another bill had turned up, at Sears Roebuck a block away.

This time the bill-passer was a grandmother buying housedresses.

And Bruce's afternoon—and Casey's, and David's—became a nightmare of responding to leads about the ransom cash and the dozens of people apparently employed to pass it.

By late in the day sufficient leads were congregating around Farmers & Merchants Bank in the Harmonia Building that Bruce and Casey sat down with its manager, Mr. Spielmann.

Spielmann, his coat on, was about to go home. Instead, he related his tale of doing an admittedly unusual favor for Thrall & Hawkins—most respectable customers of long standing— and how little trouble it was, really, and quite understandable, dealing with the Cubans. He showed Thrall's signature on the receipt.

"*Cubans*," Bruce grunted.

"Did I do something wrong?" Spielmann asked.

Casey glared. "Nothing we can put you away for."

Spielmann looked only half reassured.

Bruce let Washington know that following the trail of marked bills was useless. The ransom had been laundered— washed, as he told the Director, "squeaky clean."

## 32.

VERGIL DROVE HIS last segment even faster, from Columbus, Kentucky, speeding six miles east to U.S. 51, then nine miles north to the Indian Mounds at Wickliffe.

Two wheels left the road once and he had to wrestle them back onto the pavement. Given that crossing the river took half an hour, Vergil was confident Joe couldn't overtake him, but he pushed nonetheless. His luck held; when the Indian Mounds poked mildly into sight across the road from the WigWam Lodge, Joe was not in his mirror, nor were there any roadblocks.

He was *there* — a good eight miles south of Cairo. He jerked off the road and pulled up to the WigWam Lodge.

On their trips to see his wife's people in St. Louis, whether in summer or at Thanksgiving or Christmas, it was Thrall family custom to break the journey and explore the Indian Mounds, see what was new since last time.

The mounds themselves were modest relics of ancient Indian life that resembled the berms of a Civil War fort. To call them — as barns painted with the Great Pyramids proclaimed throughout the South — *The 8th Wonder of the Ancient World!* was grossly misleading. But Harry Thrall, like other boys, enjoyed seeing the latest arrowheads and bits of pottery dug out of the earth. And every year whoever was first to see the little bumps would rush to say, "I spy the pyramids!" And collapse in laughter.

The WigWam Lodge featured a two-story plaster teepee housing a lobby with wagon-wheel chandeliers and stone fireplace, to either side a dozen one-room cabins with carports between them. Wrecks were parked in some of the carports; the lodge proprietor also ran the local tow truck, and found them a convenient place to put the smashed and bloody cars he pulled off the roads. But Vergil was grateful as he rented a cabin and parked his Ford beside a crumpled DeSoto that helped hide it from the highway.

Once inside he breathed easier. The room, paneled in pine, boasted a gas heater and kitchenette. After hastily washing up, he moved a chair to the gauze-curtained windows. Soon — not 20 minutes later — he heard a motor working hard and saw a Ford V-8 come skittering up the road. The car positioned itself on the straightaway, expertly took the curve on its inside wheels, and vanished.

Vergil recognized Joe clutching the wheel.

JOE TOOK AT SPEED a tricky curve beside a teepee-like motor court and a billboard for *The 8th Wonder of the Ancient World!* supporting a giant red arrow aimed across the road. Even before his trained eye caught a brown Ford sitting behind a wreck, with the certainty of intuition he apprehended the full beauty of *"I spy the pyramids"* — the reference being not to Cairo, Illinois, but to the Wickliffe Mounds. He realized the WigWam Lodge was to be the ransom drop.

Might as well be hanged for a sheep as for a lamb.

Out of sight of that curve, he stopped at a little assemblage of stores and cafés that serviced the tourist traffic. Finding a telephone booth in one, he called Sturgis at Indianola Farm.

"OK, sir, I'm south of Cairo at —"

"Hey, Joe, glad you called: The Director solved your little pyramids riddle."

"He *did?*"

"Got a buck on ya? Take a look," Sturgis said. Joe found a dollar bill in his wallet. "Turn it over. See the Great Seal? Of the United States? It's a *pyramid*, genius. 'I spy' was Thrall's way of telling his son he was getting the money. We already pulled your roadblocks at Cairo. You got to get back to Memphis."

"Great," said Joe. "Just calling to tell you the ransom drop is the WigWam Lodge in Wickliffe, Kentucky."

"Your career, sport," Sturgis told him for the second time that day.

Joe hung up, unfazed and undeterred. He gassed up, bought sandwiches and coffee, and carefully positioned his car beside a Fisk tire store, where atop a column a yawning cement infant in a nightgown balanced a tire on his shoulder while holding a candle aloft over the legend, *"Time to Re-Tire."*

He could just see the Ford. If Vergil came out Joe would see him. If Harry went in Joe hoped he would see him.

If no one came or went, or not so Joe noticed, it would be time to take the little boy's advice, maybe give the bond business a try.

## 33.

THE KIDNAPPING OF Lucie Spode White jolted the nation.

It was front-page news everywhere, leading item of the radio bulletins, number one topic of conversation. The public, feeling suddenly unsafe and vulnerable, clamored for information, but was starved of it. Over and over the papers ran the same file photographs of the victim, repeated the same speculation about ransom demands.

In Falls City a theory took hold that Lucie's abductors never fled the region at all but were holding her locally, outwitting a nationwide search by the simple stratagem of sitting it out. Gangs formed to interrogate strangers, investigate neighbors' attics and break into empty cabins.

Pearl Gossamer White was of this school of thought, but Chief Eckerdt assured him nothing could be done until the kidnappers made contact. Therefore Pearl followed his usual routine when back from an out-of-town trip, ritually starting up his fire engines and running them down to the gates and back to the barn. The crowd at the gates was incredulous at the parade of gleaming engines that first came thundering down the drive, then chugged basso uphill again beneath clouds of black smoke.

The fourth he took down the hill was a particular prize, a candy-apple red 1930 American LaFrance aglimmer with brass. The crowd was appraising it with newly educated eyes when, as he turned it around, out of the corner of his eye Pearl – and Pearl alone – saw what he was sure was Lucie's bandaged head nodding on the shoulder of a brute maneuvering an Oldsmobile through the single lane the crowd reduced Falls Road to.

Nightmarish: All eyes were on him, but no one heard or could heed his cry, *"Stop that car! Get that Olds!"* even as he thought he saw it whisking his wife away.

He took action. Bawling out to open the gates, he signaled one of his men to hop aboard, wheeled west onto Falls Road and pushed the accelerator to the floor, meanwhile instructing his man to wind the siren. Already painfully far behind the Olds, the fire engine picked up speed slowly. But once it got going, urged on by the *whine-whine-whine* of the siren, its speed had a massive, unstoppable quality.

The Olds turned off Falls Road.

So did the American LaFrance.

The car's driver showed familiarity with the lanes and roads, but Pearl knew them just as well, and when the Oldsmobile found the Fontainebleau Road and stuck to it, he dogged it fully 60 miles. His vehicle was built to transport tons of water, but the water tanks were empty and twin gas tanks full; Pearl could speed all day. The sheriffs of the counties he traversed radioed ahead to clear the road: *The Spode family is trying to make contact!* Officers stood at the roadside saluting Pearl as he screamed past.

No one thought to stop the Olds.

On the outskirts of Fontainebleau from one moment to the next the car vanished—utterly. Pearl could have spit from frustration. He looked for it for a time, but had no luck and got no satisfaction barking queries down at taciturn locals. When he found a respectable house, the siren ignominiously died as he reported by telephone to the State Police. (They promised to interview the owner of every Olds in the state.)

Pearl turned his great machine around and trundled noisily home, nursing a smoking bearing in a rear wheel, dissatisfied, but withal grimly pleased with himself.

The houses he returned to seethed with frustration. Lucie's father stayed put at Indianola Farm, but there was nothing he could do to help, any more than his son-in-law next door. Separately medicating their apprehensions with Willinger's Reserve, they waited—waited to hear that the kidnappers had gotten their money and were releasing Lucie.

But no word came.

## 34.

VERGIL THRALL WATCHED steadily through the gauze curtains. He was starving, but ignored the pangs; he didn't dare stir, lest Harry drive right past.

Meanwhile the daylight died. It lasted past 7:00 o'clock, then was quenched. Darkness fell with October precipitance.

He calculated and recalculated possible travel times. His son was fortunate to have mostly flat country to traverse on a dry day, with paved Federal highways the whole way.

But he was calculating in water. He had no way of knowing when Harry might call the house, or that he would, or that *"I spy the pyramids"* would convey anything to him, even if his wife remembered to say it. But if he called and she remembered, Harry could arrive at any time—perhaps most likely, a few hours after sundown.

Where the G-Man was, he didn't know. He'd seen him pass. Would he just barrel on through for Minneapolis? Or, if he sensed Vergil no longer fleeing ahead of him, would he turn around? Stop to oversee a canvass of Cairo with the army of reinforcements he could call up with a snap of his Federal fingers? Canvass Cairo—*and* environs?

Vergil sat in the dark, quivering with tension. The headlights of every approaching car pushed the shadow of his head left or right across the walls; the shadow stretched along the paneling, trembled and snapped back as the car passed.

Hours later, his shadow stretched along the wall as a car rounded the curve from the north, but instead of snapping back it was projected to giant size as headlights turned in and came near. They flicked off, and the driver got out.

Harry!

Vergil opened his door and called, *"Harry!"*

His son—gleaming despite hours behind the wheel—strode over and put out his hand.

Vergil pulled him inside.

"You *fool.*"

"Got your message, Dad."

Vergil locked the door, suddenly angry.

"Harry, you *idiot*. What a *stupid* thing you've done. Not good, and not smart."

"Not my idea, Dad."

"Whose was it? Not your *wife's?*"

"Lucie's." Dimples and a flash of ivory. "Lucie Spode White's? We had something going when I was working for her old man? One day she's complaining how tight the purse strings are and says" — his voice went falsetto — "'Kidnap me, Harry, they'll pay a hundred grand and we'll split it.'"

"*Good God.*" His father collapsed onto the edge of the bed, next to the Gladstone bag. "That means—"

" —there's no crime. Smart girl, huh? Tricking her own family out of her own money? Nothing they can do to *her*, and since I'm in it with her, nothing they can do to *me*. This the ransom?" Harry lifted the bag.

Vergil looked at his son's handsome, confident face, and once again felt he was spying on Earth from the perspective of the gods: *What fools ye mortals be!*

"Hope you're right, Harry. There's no crime, except *my* taking their cash, *my* fibbing to Federal agents, *my* abetting *you*.

"But how's it going to work out for *you?* You can't expect the woman to volunteer it was *her* idea. No, she'll have a harrowing tale to tell — about *you!*

"And whom will they believe? You're up against the *Spodes*, my boy. That's a dangerous neighborhood. They play for *keeps*."

"If it's so dangerous, maybe I should keep it all?" Harry hefted the bag with a grin.

"*No!* My God, son, your only hope is to keep her happy. She's your ace in the hole."

"So don't worry," laughed Harry. "No mistakes so far. And thanks for the swag."

His father watched him open the bag's jaws and plunge his

hands into greenbacks with the same greedy gesture as his mother gathering chrysanthemums — was it only yesterday?

"Wish I knew if they were marked."

"They're not," Vergil wearily assured him. "It's cold money, my bank exchanged it."

"What an old Dad!"

"Where do you have her, Harry?"

"Now, Dad."

"But is she all right?"

"She's *fine*. Full of beans."

"Harry, best thing you can do is let her go, turn yourself in and — "

Grinning, Harry kissed his father's forehead.

"Thanks, Dad. You've been swell."

He closed the bag.

"Harry, an F.B.I. agent chased me up here," Vergil said. "I lost him, but there might be roadblocks at Cairo. Black Ford V-8. Saw him pass, don't know where he went. But you have to hurry. *Hurry.*"

## 35.

HARRY SAW THE sleepy infant atop the Fisk Tire column and yawned sympathetically, pitying his own weariness, until the sight in his mirror of a car folding in behind him snapped him alert. Making the turn east onto U.S. 60, Harry watched his mirror. The other car turned also.

Being followed was nerve-wracking, but as time passed and night deepened and traffic thinned out almost to nothing, there was something companionable in having the twin headlamps in his mirror pushing him along.

Harry didn't like driving at night. It was perilous. Roads lacked shoulders, nor were there any but center stripes, and not always those; just staying on the pavement was a challenge when the coupé seemed to outrun its headlights at 35 miles an hour. It was natural for a driver finding another going his way to pair up impromptu and pioneer together through the darkness.

*Glad of the escort,* Harry jeered. Sure, he was carrying cash — an energizing hundred grand — but it was clean cash no Spode ever touched. And there's no crime in being rich. In *America?* Where the crime is being *poor?*

Harry again entertained the notion of keeping the whole sum — of going West with twice the grubstake. (Of course he meant to head for California.)

But even if he was nothing to Lucie, he wanted her to know that he was a gentleman and man of his word. Every bit as good as she was — at *least.*

Besides, as his Dad pointed out, she was his alibi, his get-out-of-jail-free card. And with G-Men pressing from behind, an alibi might be useful — even essential. The G-Men he could evade, he felt pretty sure, but no sense being stupid and alienating Lucie to boot. So, all right, between the requirements of honor and safety, driving back to Indy was worth the all-nighter — worth $50,000.

*What larks!* he thought, this time with a certain grim irony.

Up to him to stay free. But free he would be.

Oh, free of Mabel, too. She would rue her retirement from Woolworth's — if she wanted to eat. Didn't she know there was a Depression on? Let her try her *pregnant* trick on some other sucker.

## 36.

MABEL, LEFT IN CHARGE at the apartment, felt uneasy all day and night. By herself she didn't dare feed Lucie or empty her pail—didn't dare open that closet door. But she worried that Lucie at any moment could make a ruckus, force her to do—she didn't know what.

So she stayed indoors, radio low, paging through her magazines, daring only to cook up a hamburger.

Lucie realized that Mabel was standing guard alone.

She took stock. Her entire inventory: One human body, strained beyond endurance, hungry, thirsty, exhausted and foul, clad in silk dingy and soiled. Pearl necklace and earrings. High heels. A filthy wooden bucket. Nothing metal beyond bobbie pins and her garters' and jewelry's tiny clasps. She had nothing, in other words, but her desperate need to get out of that closet.

One crazy idea alone presented itself: Lure Mabel to open the door, toss a handful of pearls at her and, as Mabel desperately tap danced to keep her balance, dash past to freedom.

She broke the strand and poured the pearls into a shoe. With tiny taps a few dropped to the floor.

"Miss?" she called. Again: *"Lady?* Lady, are you *there?"*

No answer, but she sensed unease.

"I'm hungry, Lady! Lady, I need something to eat!"

She kept it up for five minutes, but Mabel never responded.

Then Lucie took the other shoe and pounded at the door.

Mabel immediately approached, with nervous authority saying, "Stop that noise this *instant."*

"I'm hungry," said Lucie.

"Lookit, girlie, want your nice money, just hang on. Harry'll be back in the morning."

Lucie hit the door with her shoe twice more, then stopped.

She remembered a phrase from somewhere: *long night of the soul.* Closing her eyes, she imagined herself lying in her own big bed at home. She curled up on the floor—there wasn't room to stretch out—and clapped her hands to her ears. Trees rustled outside her windows, and the river flowed.

Harry was acting on her idea. She admitted that. It was an idea she'd nurtured lovingly, an idea worth $50,000 to her. A lovely, easy idea.

So there she was. Locked in a closet, counting on this *idiot*—on *Dimples*—to evade a nation on the alert for him and then present her with half the loot!

Who was the stupid one here?

Yet—

Yet maybe he'd pull it off. Bring her $50,000—cash.

All that money. Well, it would make up for a lot.

Where was he, anyway?

## 37.

HARRY STUDIED HIS rearview mirror. If that car stayed on his tail he'd have to figure something out in Indianapolis, some way to get her share to his partner in crime.

In Henderson, Kentucky he stopped for gas and a sandwich. He was amused to see the other car gassing up across the street at the competing all-night station. It was a black Ford V-8, a far faster car than his. He nodded at its driver, who not only smiled in return but snapped a jaunty little wave. Harry was surprised there was only the one of them.

The trip resumed, and they ran thus all night. Traffic was scanty, the very occasional approach of headlights a major event.

Hours later, at Terre Haute, Harry stopped again for gas and to stretch his legs. He was exhausted—running first all day, now all night, and even a young man's nervous energy ebbs in the hours before dawn, when everything fleshly drags to earth. The sleepy gas jockey pushed the hose in the tank, and Harry stumbled towards the station's clapboard annex, an all-night diner with a row of revolving stools lined up before a counter.

A drunk slurping coffee already presided at the near end. Harry sat down in the middle. As he ordered coffee and lemon pie, keeping a watchful eye on his car, he saw the Ford pull up behind his Chevy.

Obviously it needed gas, too, and there was no place else to get it. Harry saw its driver get out, stretch, speak to the attendant and unconcernedly saunter over to the diner.

Nodding at Harry as he passed him, Joe took the far end and ordered a slab of cherry pie with coffee.

"Hey, friend," said Harry.

Joe turned and said, "Hey. Dark night, isn't it?"

"Oh yeah. Where you headed?"

"Indianapolis," said Joe without hesitation.

"Me, too," Harry said with a quick smile. "Just had to pull off a while."

"Me, too."

They interrogated each other—Joe said he was an accounting clerk, Harry that he was a traveling salesman—and enjoyed each other's lies. (The drunk chimed in that he was in hardware.) At first both were tense, but soon they relaxed into a punchy suspension of themselves. Each knew the score, thought he knew it better than the other, was tired to boot. Drama might come at the end of their journey, but was not permitted inside the diner.

Harry bragged about the hot number he was rushing to meet, a girl who would do it any time, anywhere, any way he wanted it. Joe said he had a girl, too, drumming his shoe against the foot rail as he chastely described Miss Willis. (The drunk advised caution with women.) Their manner had the amorous charm and feminine grace of young men on those rare occasions when, on the implicit condition that combat will resume at the first opportunity, they declare a truce and let down their guards.

Each accepted a refill from the waitress and scraped his plate clean of crumbs.

Harry insisted on paying both checks, and conspicuously over-tipped.

"Enjoy your drive," he commanded Joe, dimpling and offering his hand.

"Hey, thanks," said Joe, shaking firmly. "And thanks for the pie!"

Harry was paying for the gas as Joe walked past with another smile and a glance that discerned the Gladstone bag in Harry's passenger seat.

He showed no reaction, but vindication surged through his veins: He'd risked *everything*, chasing Vergil Thrall and staking out the motel, then not taking Harry red-handed with the money but trailing him to the victim—risked *everything* on Spode's Gladstone bag resting on the seat.

He could have arrested Harry then and there, but Lucie was the thing—the victim had to be his foremost consideration. There was less risk to her in letting her kidnapper return to her as, for reasons unknown, he appeared to be doing, than in arresting him and hoping he would tell him where she was. And the laundering of the cash made an arrest now problematical at best.

The coupé nudged towards the road and paused on its verge. Joe followed. Harry making a feint of pulling out, Joe took the bait and smoothly pulled past him.

Harry followed — *laughing!* — and stayed close as Joe drove east, Indy straight ahead, hanging back only far enough to dip his headlights politely below Joe's mirror. The night was alive around them, the new day stirring just across the horizon. They rode onwards, watching the cones of their headlights cede power to the first gray daylight.

At a little farm town they came upon a Victorian manse with sail-like slate roofs. Joe in his half-consciousness, awake a second night running, trying to figure out how to get back behind that Chevy following him, admired over the hedge a lifelike iron stag. He failed to notice how very lifelike it was until too late, when the deer leaped the hedge, landed in front of him and froze.

He smashed into it.

Its back broken, the stag slid up the hood and shattered the windshield, showering Joe with shards of glass and pinioning him with its antlers. Though he couldn't budge two inches, he managed to keep the car on the pavement, finally to stop it.

By supreme effort he got out from under the dying deer and kicked his way out of the wreck. He was covered in blood — mostly the stag's, but his face was beribboned with cuts, too.

The Chevy pulled up in the other lane. Harry leaned across and asked, "You OK, friend?"

"Think so," Joe answered. "But my car's had it."

"Oh, too bad," said Harry, and scooted off braying his klaxon: *A-OOH-GA! A-OOH-GA!* It taunted Joe for half a mile:

*A-OOH-GA!*

Joe ran furiously after him, dashed his hat to the ground, kicked the Ford and kicked the deer. Then he dragged the animal by its back legs onto the shoulder and checked the car's damage. A fender had gouged a tire, left it flat. Worse, the radiator was split, hot water dribbling out. He pushed the Ford off the road. A litter of blood and glass remained on the roadway, but he couldn't do anything about that.

By luck, another car, a Chrysler—a white convertible, yet, top up, with red leather seats—came along not much later.

Joe stood in its path, holding out his badge. It stopped, and Joe informed the driver that the Federal government was commandeering his vehicle. The driver—a doctor returning home to that very manse after a difficult childbirth—said it was doing no such thing. Finally Joe had to haul him out and send him sprawling, his bag spilling instruments and pills across the pavement.

Joe drove off, steering the Chrysler around broken glass to the doctor's enraged imprecations against that Bolshevik, Franklin Delano Roosevelt.

Joe pushed the accelerator. Everything depended on his catching up to Harry. The egg on his face if, after chasing him all night, he lost him and failed to rescue Lucie would make an omelet big enough to feed the entire Bureau.

And then some, he realized: For he'd failed to tell the doctor to telephone Sturgis and alert the Indianapolis police to the Chevy. Well, no time now. Telephone poles ratcheted past in mockery as the Chrysler skimmed along cornfields ready for harvest. As the sun rose the fields passed through tints of brown and gold.

Then he had the Chevy in sight again.

He hung back so as not to present a familiar silhouette in the unfamiliar vehicle as they began to negotiate Indianapolis's outskirts. Stoplights caught Harry a few times, but Joe worked closer by running them. At Monument Circle Harry turned up North Meridian and soon was slowing at a Spanish-style apartment house and turning down an alleyway.

Seeing the Chevy enter an old stable, Joe pulled to the curb at the next corner, beside a storekeeper sweeping his sidewalk.

He showed his badge and got on the phone to Indianola Farm.

## 38.

HARRY MOVED FAST, for all that he thought he'd outrun his pursuer.

Bag in hand, he unlocked his apartment door and walked through living room and bedroom — where Mabel was snoring away — to the closet, turned its key and opened the door wide.

Lucie seized awake on the floor. The stench made Harry step back and wrinkle his nose in repugnance, which she noticed as she scrabbled to her hands like an animal.

"OK, Toots," he whispered. "Here's your half."

Dropping the bag, he squatted beside it and started hauling out packets of bills.

The bills were a mix of 20s, tens, fives and ones. He did the best he could, as fast as he could, to split the haul evenly. In the event he piled up $48,325 in front of her and retained $51,675 in the bag. Lucie's mouth worked, her eyes widened at sight of the cash, but she articulated nothing more than a whisper Harry didn't bother to catch.

"Got to fly, Lucie. It's been fun. Remember, mum's the

word, or I spill it was *your* idea."

Mabel suddenly sat up.

"You got it, Harry, you really got it? That's grand!"

"She needs a bath awful bad, Mabel," Harry told her. "Help her get cleaned up, won't you?"

He waited as Mabel eagerly got out of bed and started running the tub.

Then he left.

In the converted stable was a decrepit-looking but sturdy Dodge pickup truck that belonged to another tenant, a retired farmer who, Harry happened to know, drove it only on weekends. Cranking the engine alive, he was driving down the alley before Joe was off the telephone.

At Monument Circle he turned west on U.S. 40 – the same road he'd just come in on – and headed for Illinois. Taking the truck gave him some time – he hoped enough. Only someone who recognized its weekday absence as unusual could identify the Dodge as his getaway vehicle. It would happen, but likely not for hours. Time enough to slip through any dragnet.

## 39.

THE SIGHT AND SMELL and touch of money soon restored Lucie to herself.

As soon as Harry was gone, and while Mabel was still in the bathroom, she found her handbag and took Mabel's bigger one from on top of the dresser and filled both with the larger bills. The $1 bills – a couple thousand, all told – she piled on the bed, and spilled the shoeful of pearls beside them. When Mabel came out, Lucie told her they were hers in gratitude for her kindness, then dipped herself in the tub.

"You shouldn't have!" Mabel was still squealing after Lucie had patted herself dry and pulled on a dowdy print dress of Mabel's she grabbed at random. It was like dressing up in the kind of floral wallpaper that hides the dirt. "Thank you, dear," Mabel was saying. "Did what I could, but you know Harry. Now what? Where are you going, dear? That's *my* purse."

"I need it," Lucie explained, pressing both bulging handbags to her sides and heading for the door. "I know my way."

She pushed into the hallway. Stuffing her singles and pearls in a paper sack, Mabel scrambled after.

JOE WOKE UP Melvin Sturgis with the news that, ransom in hand, the kidnapper was apparently returning to his victim, named the street corner where the Chrysler idled and said he would reconnoiter until the cops appeared.

"Dammit, can't you hold him for *me?*" Sturgis snapped. "I could be there in—"

"Can't wait, might be on the move."

Joe hung up, leaving Sturgis to call the local force, and cautiously approached the apartment house. He found the Chevy, but it was empty. People were coming out to go to work, but Harry wasn't among them.

He knocked at the door of the resident manager, a hard-bitten woman in a bathrobe whose husband, a casualty of the Great War, repeatedly invited Joe to feel the hole in his head.

Her face softened as Joe asked if she knew Harry Thrall.

"Oh, yes, we like Mr. Thrall," she answered. "Salesman, out of work. His wife Mabel lives there, too. Honeymooners—if you catch my drift. Don't run a monastery here, even if their neighbor thinks I should. That's apartment 27. I'll show you."

She plucked a key from a pegboard and, still in slippers, shuffled upstairs from her cellar quarters. At number 27's door she knocked with a landlady's peremptoriness and inserted her key, but was surprised to find the door unlocked.

The apartment was empty.

LUCIE MARCHED SIX BLOCKS north, Mabel following as she turned into the parsonage next to the Capitol Methodist Episcopal Church. Behind them, police sirens began to converge.

Lucie rang while Mabel, trying to think what to do, stuck to her side.

A maid pulled the door open.

"Hello, Betty," said Lucie. "Is Father Gray in?"

Father Gray at his breakfast table was astonished to look up from the headlines— ***"WHERE'S LUCIE? FLORIDA TOWN TURNED UPSIDE DOWN!"***—to see Lucie Spode White walk in with another woman. He was an old family friend, her father's roommate at Lawrenceville.

When Lucie refused his offer of fried eggs, or any food at all, he sat her down in his study and they called Indianola Farm. Her first thought was of her father, not her husband. She kept both handbags on her lap.

To Lucie's father's very great surprise, half an hour after Joe's call to Sturgis electrified the household and led to a flurry of telephoning between Washington, Falls City and Indianapolis, he found himself talking to his daughter.

"Are you *free*, Lucie? Are you all *right?*"

Lucie considered and said, "Yes, Father, I'm free. I'm fine but tired. *Very* tired. I want to come home."

Rev. Gray took the telephone.

"Bob, my machine can be ready in five minutes. I'll drive her myself."

*"Will* you, Sam?"

Lucie parted from Mabel outdoors.

"Mabel, you were kind to me. You've nothing to worry about."

"Well, I tried, it's my Christian duty, but Harry kept—"

Father Gray backed his Hudson out of the garage, Lucie got in and they left Mabel behind.

MABEL HURRIED HOME.

Her pace slowed at sight of the policemen already ringing the building. When a young man with cuts on his face, not in uniform, suddenly strode towards her, she made as if to turn around.

"Mabel Thrall?" asked Joe Albright.

"Yes?"

"You're under arrest."

"But I didn't *dooo* anything," she wailed as he opened her paper bag to find it filled with pearls and dollar bills.

"Then you have nothing to worry about," he offered, handcuffing her.

AFTER HARRY LEFT him, Vergil Thrall went to bed, but was unable to sleep. All night he lay worrying about his son. About his son, but also about himself: He was now certainly an accessory, though not, apparently, to a crime. Except the point could be argued.

He had to hope Harry got away with it, because any alternative was grim. Harry had to bring Lucie her half of the ransom and vanish. Were he forced to explain the kidnapping as a cooperative venture between Lucie and himself, the fruit of their affair, the Spodes would eat him alive. He would never see daylight again, and might well get the Chair. His supposed ace in the hole? A deep, black hole; all hole and no ace.

And for himself, no clear deliverance either, unless the Spodes were inclined to quash the whole matter. And he knew better than that. Harry might vanish forever, and his dad still end up in prison.

Vergil thus fretted as day dawned and there came a knock on his door. It repeated itself urgently, but he didn't move. He had no intention of answering it.

There was no need to. The door crashed open and five bulky figures burst in and aimed pistols.

"Vergil Thrall? You're under arrest."

## 40.

FATHER GRAY'S AUTOMOBILE was making good time down U.S. 31. He was concerned at Lucie's reserve, but her days in the closet forever deprived her of her hallmark spontaneity, replacing it with a mechanism of delay — a second, or two or three, that preceded any response.

He suggested they stop so she could eat, but Lucie, after a few moments, pleaded her wish to get home.

They were speeding on when, near Scottsburg, they encountered a roadblock: Police cars suddenly moved onto the pavement in front of them, and to either side marksmen stepped out of the cornfields aiming rifles.

"*What the –!*" The priest squealed to a stop. Terrified, Lucie shrank back.

Melvin Sturgis stepped out of Pearl White's Cadillac cradling a Tommy gun.

"Sturgis, F.B.I.," he announced. "Mrs. White? This way,

please."

"I have to go, Father Gray," said Lucie. "Thank you so much."

"God be with you, my child."

Sturgis handed Lucie into the Cadillac's backseat.

"Move over," he told her. Sitting down next to her, he commanded the driver, *"Go!"*

They roared off with a State Police motorcycle escort, sirens wailing.

Sturgis inspected Lucie from head to toe.

"Welcome back, Mrs. White," he said. "You OK?"

Lucie considered.

"Fine," she answered.

"They treat you all right?"

She thought about it.

"Yes," she reported.

He regarded her. Each elbow pinned a purse to her ribs.

*"Two* purses, Mrs. White?"

As his words percolated into her consciousness she gaped at him and held on tighter.

But Sturgis reached out and wrested the nearer one from beneath her arm and opened it. He seemed unsurprised to find it crammed with money. She gave him a dirty look.

"Now the other," he said, reaching. She burrowed into the corner but, grunting with effort, Sturgis took the other purse away from her, too.

It, too, overflowed with cash.

"Well, well, well," he said, low. He weighed them and glanced at his driver, whose head was facing strictly forward. "Surprised at you, Mrs. White, I surely am. Finding all this money on you leads to an inescapable conclusion. Wouldn't want your Daddy to know what you've been up to, would you?" Looking at her, he repeated, *"Inescapable."*

Watching the scenery, Lucie said nothing. Cornfields were giving way to the southern Indiana knobs.

"But maybe we can come to an arrangement." She didn't answer. "How about one for you and one for me? *That's* fair, isn't it?"

He placed the lighter purse in her lap, opened a briefcase at his feet, dumped the contents of the heavier into it, rolled down his window and tossed out the empty handbag. One of the motorcycle outriders swerved to avoid it, briefly touching a foot to the pavement before resuming his upright posture.

In the middle of the Qwattata River bridge, motorcyclists of the Falls City Police smoothly replaced the Indiana escort. A few miles up Falls Road, Sturgis halted the motorcade and, with apologies to Lucie, abandoned the backseat and took his place on the running board. Drawing his .38 Special and angling back his hat, he struck a heroic pose as the wailing vehicles threaded the reporters and onlookers at the gates of Overridge.

"That's Melvin Sturgis!"

Flashbulbs popped at the famous head.

"My God, and there's Lucie!"

"*Lucie!* It's *Lucie!* Lucie Spode White, right there!"

Sturgis was permitting himself a smile at the enthusiasm when his driver, misjudging the rate at which the crowd gave way, bashed into a gatepost and scraped a fender. Naturally, the photograph that graced front pages coast-to-coast that evening showed Sturgis grimacing, off-balance, Lucie behind him clutching a fat handbag.

"Lucie, say something!" yelled a reporter.

She smiled, held it until it soured, renewed it and said, "What's a little paint off a fender at a time like this?"

And rode on, smile clenched, to the house.

## 41.

"I'M FINE, I'M FINE," Lucie assured her husband, father, Bessie Longworth, Lily Willis and everybody else. "*Fine*. But so tired."

All she wanted was a bath and bed, but already a celebration was starting up downtown. Everybody—her husband above all—knew a great, one-time-only blow-out was required.

Even as Lucie was riding home, Pearl set the preparations in train. Conferring with his father-in-law and the manager of the River House, he issued a spate of orders, wrote a bevy of checks and set Miss Bryant to telephoning the cream of Falls City society with invitations to the most lavish party seen in the hotel's Spode Ballroom since the Crash.

But when, at his first embrace, Pearl told her about it, Lucie was aghast.

"What *I* want is a bath," she repeated, "and after my bath I want to sleep as long as I can."

Bessie ran her bath and Lucie adjourned upstairs to take it. A long bath; the family—popping champagne corks and discussing menus downstairs—became nervous as to its length. She soaked languidly in a cloud of bubbles, occasionally renewing the hot water, while Bessie arranged her clothes in the dressing room.

"Lawdy, treated you *cruel*, giving you *curtains* to wear," Bessie called. "But you be over it soon."

Lucie heard the snap of a handbag and an intake of breath.

"Miss Lucie, *where* in Sam Hill you get all this *money*?"

Soapy and dripping, Lucie was suddenly beside her, tearing the purse out of her hands, tossing it in a drawer and locking the drawer.

"Bessie, no questions."

Bessie opened her mouth.

"I *said*, no questions."

"Yes'm," Bessie said quietly.

Lucie padded back to the tub.

Eventually conceding she was clean, she emerged from the water and went to bed. Getting clean and getting some sleep were big items in the list of things she had to do. But two or three items remained.

She ticked off the next after her husband tenderly knocked at the door. The sight of Pearl in his tuxedo, ready to go to the ball, and the thought of what she now had to undergo horrified her. But she had to endure it.

"Oh Pearl . . . You don't have to go *this minute*, I hope?"

Pleased, he folded her, moist and powdered, in his arms.

"Promise you, Lucie, we'll burn the men who took you, unless I get my hands on 'em first, and then we'll do it the old-fashioned way, tie 'em to a tree and cut off—"

"Oh Pearl, you can't imagine how good it is to see you."

Actually, Pearl's ego (male) allowed him an even possibly exaggerated idea of her gladness. He was surprised only that, having thus seduced him, even having unrolled the lambskin herself, Lucie proved so unresponsive. Lay there like a dead fish, in fact. But it was not the time to complain.

Having done his duty, and she firm in her refusal to accompany him—despite his offer to take her into town enthroned in a fire engine—Pearl trotted out to his Cadillac. Lucie meanwhile shrouded herself in her bedclothes as in a tent, a mug of hot cocoa in her hands, two of Chief Eckerdt's men flanking her door.

DESPITE LUCIE'S ABSENCE from her own homecoming, America took her to its heart that evening; the 300 invited to the Spode Ballroom celebrated raucously.

CBS Radio carried the affair via remote broadcast, sponsored by Willinger's, which introduced its saucy new slogan, *Bottoms Up with Willinger's Reserve!* Bourbon flowed like the Qwattata River, while not one but two dance bands played. By chance Glenn Miller was in the middle of an engagement at The Spode, and the new song he tossed off dedicated to Lucie — *The Girl Worth Every Penny* — was a smash. Artie Shaw's Orchestra was appearing at French Lick, but the casino loaned it for the broadcast, and on the bus down Shaw came up with a version of *I Found a Million Dollar Baby (in a Five and Ten Cent Store)* that had the ballroom rocking.

The Spodes and their closest friends danced and caroused and drank, while outdoors the unwashed throngs pressed up against police barricades, eating free hot dogs and dancing to music piped from the ballroom.

Lucie's father and Pearl White made brief, tongue-tied speeches, conveying their gratitude and Lucie's regrets. Everybody understood her nonappearance; it was not every day in Falls City that a Spode received such sympathy.

The ballroom fell silent as a radio statement by J. Edgar Hoover from F.B.I. Headquarters was announced. There was a fascinating interval of dead air — the ballroom, bannered and ballooned, went suddenly ethereal and weird and self-conscious. Then Hoover's precise speech broke in. He congratulated the men of his Bureau and expressed gratitude to them — especially to Special Agent Melvin Sturgis — for returning the lost little lady to the bosom of her family. He promised that his men would soon nab the miscreant Harry Thrall, whose description he provided, indeed lingered over, and added his best wishes for Lucie.

CBS signed off, and the music and dancing resumed. By the time competing swing renditions of *Auld Lang Syne* ended the ball, Pearl was roaring drunk. Chief Eckerdt assigned a squad car to get him home safely (Pearl's own driver having celebrated overmuch), and at Overridge they carried him in and deposited him on the bed next to his wife. By mistake; they couldn't know that *his* bedroom was down the hall.

After snoring for some hours Pearl showed signs of stirring. Lucie got up and stole with a hatpin into his bathroom, where he kept his supply of condoms in a cedar drawer. Carefully she pierced each package. The holes were invisible, but fingers could feel the puckering where the pin went through.

"Pearl!" she screamed.

He lumbered in, his broad face creased in sleep. She held out a foil.

"Pearl, it's been tampered with! They *all* have! Oh, and I so wanted—"

And that was that.

Of course she was pregnant. She would carry it, bear it, raise it as the young prince or princess of the Spodes. There was no alternative.

She never made love to her husband again—or to any man.

She and Pearl forthwith closed up Overridge forever, that very day discharging Bessie, Bertram and the other staff, and before nightfall flying to New York.

Two days later they sailed for Le Havre. After sojourning that winter in the south of France, they cruised the Mediterranean, rented an abbey in Wiltshire, and returned to her father's house, where she gave birth to a bedimpled heir she named Robert Spode White.

## 42.

ABOUT THE TIME Melvin Sturgis' car was bashing into a gatepost, Harry Thrall was coming upon the farm town of Effingham, Illinois.

Seeing a used-car lot trimmed with pennants, he turned around and drove back to the park he'd passed outside town, where a field of picnic tables sloped down to a river overhung by trees. Making sure he was alone, he placed the Gladstone bag on the grass, rolled down the truck's windows and gently pushed it into the river. The mud on the bank sucked at its tires, slowing its roll, but eventually it rumbled into the water until only a corner of the roof challenged the surface. Then, the current tugging, even that dipped from sight.

Harry carried his bag back to the car lot. Among the autos for sale was a maroon Model A that appeared to have some life left in it. Soon it was Harry's, though he signed the bill of sale John Simons.

And like that, he was free — free, rich and on the open road.

A burst of energy took him by mid-afternoon to Vandalia. Parking off the street, he took a hotel room and went to bed. He fell asleep with his hand delving the riches of the Gladstone bag under the covers with him. Waking up next morning profoundly refreshed, he put in a long day's driving.

In Lawrence, Kansas, he finally indulged himself, trading in the Model A for a handsome new green Buick 60 and went on his way West. Drinking a cup of coffee in Larned, Kansas, he picked up a girl named Julia Breese and drove on with her to California.

Thus did Harry Thrall, proclaimed by the F.B.I. Public

Enemy Number One — he remained so until dislodged by the Karpis Gang — beat what the New York *Times* called *The Charge of the 'G' Brigade*. For weeks dark-haired, dimpled young men in places as far-flung as Tampa, Dayton and Seattle were made to explain themselves, or even arrested — even jailed. A month into the manhunt, based on a soda jerk's purported encounter in Moline, Illinois, J. Edgar Hoover issued a hysterical all-points bulletin warning that Harry might have disguised himself as a woman calling herself "Mrs. S. Manley."

But the F.B.I. couldn't find Mrs. Manley, either.

SHORTLY AFTER HARRY THRALL vanished, J. Edgar Hoover summoned Joe Albright to Washington. Joe looked bleakly out the train windows the whole way, as if hoping Harry would climb on board and join him.

In Hoover's enormous office at the Department of Justice, Joe stood at attention some yards short of the desk. Hoover, dressed in a bold checked suit, steamed silently for some time, while to the side his deputy (and housemate) Clyde Tolson — clad in the identical loud suit — washed Joe with cold, cold eyes.

Then Hoover let loose.

"*Never* has one of my agents fucked up *so* bad, chatting over a nice piece of *pie* with a *kidnapper* who proceeds to give him the *slip* in the wilds of a major metropolitan *city* — "

"Yes, sir."

Hoover pulsated with rage.

"A *coffeeklatsch* with your *boyfriend* sounds very *sweet* — don't it, Clyde? — but if the public *ever* finds out about it — !"

"Sir, I'm sorry — "

"*Sorry* don't cut it, Albright. We're going to punish your sorry ass: You'll rue the day you joined my Bureau, promise you that!"

Joe gulped, and Tolson spoke up.

"Transferring you to a certain rough little burg by the name of Loss-*angle*-ease." Joe had never heard of it, momentarily despaired, until he realized he meant *Los Angeles*. "Down and dirty, hot as the desert and full of Chinks, Nips, Mex and nigs. But keep your nose clean, we might not fire you."

"Thank you, sir."

Hoover glared.

"But you ever—*ever*—let a Public Enemy Number One slip through your fingers *again—!*"

Beyond fury, Hoover wheezed and gasped as Joe slowly, slowly shuffled backwards out of the presence.

"Yes, sir, I won't, sir, I promise, sir, never, sir, thank you, sir."

THE GOVERNMENT SOON separately tried Vergil Thrall and Mabel Thrall under the Lindbergh Law for aiding and abetting a kidnapping. The penalty each faced, if convicted, was death.

At trial, however, Mabel quoted Lucie praising her kindness, and was not rebutted, and Vergil claimed that, plunged willy-nilly into a crime he knew nothing about beforehand, he first acted at the government's request, and for the rest did as any father would, and both were acquitted.

The Spodes let it be known they thought justice misserved in Vergil's case. Both suffered, regardless. Mabel couldn't find work, and his late partner's son compelled Vergil to sell out his interest in the firm for a pittance, forcibly retiring him.

## III.   Eighteen months later
## May 11, 1936

## 43.

IN HOLLYWOOD, when you wake up, who are you?

He tried to remember as his wind-up Big Ben trilled itself mute in the darkness. Outdoors, birdsong enshrouded the neighborhood.

It came to him. Both the reality and the pretense.

Yawning, he leapt to his feet, put coffee on and went back to the bedroom to wake up Julia.

"Hey, baby, time to get up!"

Julia moaned tragically, turned over on her back, covered her pout with arms and pillows, and from beneath them said in a little-girl voice, "Jack, I'm *sleepy*."

"Early bird gets the worm." He pulled her toe, but she kicked.

"Cut it *out*. Staying home today."

"Julia, to play this game —"

That set her off. She sat up and tossed pillows.

"So I can't take *one day* off? Look, Jack, you've got more dimples than Clark Gable, but you're not getting anywhere either. It's rigged!"

He didn't want an argument. "Suit yourself, babe."

"Kiss my ass, Jack!"

He bathed and shaved and dressed with care. After eating breakfast, and getting a last encouraging glance from his mirror, he flicked a jacaranda blossom off the hood of his Buick and drove down Manzanita, across Sunset to Hyperion, to Riverside, and eventually reached Warner's in the San Fernando Valley.

He'd stopped off at Central Casting at Hollywood and Western on the way home the day before to get his assignment. The setting sun threw long, animated shadows from the actors—the movie extras—scrambling off a Red Car trolley as he parked and, walking with a snap to his wrists, went indoors, as always glancing up at the cast-cement nudes gracing the façade. One day he counted 76 breasts and 31 male members. Some law of irony decreed that the Central Casting building should also house the Hays Office—the movie censors, tense and celibate products of Jesuit schools. Jack presumed they pulled their hat brims low as they entered beneath all that flesh.

He'd submitted his name to Sophie at her barred window and grinned as she checked her clipboards. She usually found work for him. A young, dashing-looking guy was what the studios wanted most days, though Jack had to admit the town was crawling with handsome, well-set-up youths with miraculously clear complexions. That was why he wasn't getting *lines*, too much competition.

"You're in luck, Jack," Sophie told him. "Warner's got Cagney in a kidnapping flick, they need toughs." She looked up with sudden misgiving.

Scowling, he growled, "Right up my alley, Doll Face."

She giggled, handed him a card and said, "Warner's,

Stage 12, 8:00 a.m." and he was off.

Even without Julia—working together, they were often put in high-society nightclub scenes—he enjoyed his day, though he didn't get lines. The director sat him in a chair reading a newspaper on a set representing a tavern's back room, a spunky heiress—the kidnapping victim—tied up in a chair nearer the camera, and when Cagney looked in to ask, "How's she doin'?" another extra got the line and day-player's extra stipend: "Still kickin', boss!"

Jack knew he could have handled it, but that was the picture business for you. He thought it too dark, also, for him to be reading the paper, but that's what they wanted. Irene Dunne played the heiress. When opportunity arose at a break Jack gave her one of his frank looks, but was not unduly miffed that she ignored it.

After work he had a drink with colleagues at the Formosa Cafe, and swung by Central Casting to pick up the next day's assignment, but it was still full daylight when he returned home. Sprinklers drizzled over the lawns, and blossoms splashed purple shadows over the stucco of the Spanish-style houses.

He was happy. Having a good time. Getting tired of his girl, of course, but that happens, and other possibilities abounded—even if Irene Dunne had crossed herself off the list. And if pictures weren't going to make him a star, he might switch to something that would let him sleep in a little himself: real estate.

The Depression was still on, but in Los Angeles you hardly knew it. Already in Jack's year and a half there, the bean fields on the way to Metro had begun to sprout houses. No, he sensed money could be made in California real estate. Might be time to start turning his savings into land, especially over on the west side where the stars were moving. Had his eye on some lots off

Las Palmas.

So as he turned into the driveway and walked up the steps into his house, he was mulling the idea of moving from his take-it-as-it-comes kind of life to one more concerned with the future.

In the living room, whose arched window took in the Los Angeles basin from ocean mists at Santa Monica to the *Hollywoodland* sign strung across a scrubby hillside, Julia sat on the Mission couch.

"Hey, babe," Jack said with a smile.

His smile faded as she raised the gun from her lap.

## 44.

AFTER JACK LEFT that morning, Julia went back to sleep for an hour, then arose in leisurely fashion. While the coffee warmed up she smoked a Lucky Strike at the table in the garden.

This California, with its year-round outdoor living—what was Kansas about, anyway? Who wants to live where, when you drive to the far horizon, what you see is only a farther one?

Kansas was where she met John Simons. *If* that was his name. She'd been looking out the window of the six-stool café in Larned, across the tracks from the grain elevator her father ran, when a Buick came purring through and turned in. John Simons stepped out to stretch his legs and have a cup of coffee and piece of pie.

She poured him the coffee.

He gave her a look, got one in return. Casting a sardonic

glance at the surrounding wheat fields, he said, "Guess you must like wheat, huh?"

She blushed. He told her he was headed for Hollywood, asked if she wanted to come along. She said she might as well, dropped her apron, called into the kitchen that she'd be back in a minute and got in the car.

She was 19 and drying up in Kansas. Nineteen was old enough to make up her own mind. Wasn't like he kidnapped her or anything.

The year and a half with Jack had been fun, but now she was going on 21, in a town where every second girl was gorgeous and trying to claw her way into pictures. Where it seemed vertical progress on the career ladder was best made horizontally. She had no problem with that, if that was the way it was. But it meant Jack was almost more of a hindrance than a help.

*Almost.* After all, he did have an income, a lifesaver since extra work was hit or miss.

What she needed was a stake of her own, something to let her give, say, five years—the first half of her 20s—to the unremitting pursuit of what they weren't handing out on silver platters.

Fine for *Jack* to play at it, but she couldn't afford to. In five years she'd be going on *26*, poised atop the downslope of a woman's looks. She saw the girls working the diner counters, saw how it drained them and aged them even as they still made the rounds before or after their shifts, pestered agents, propositioned casting directors.

In Bullock's Wilshire, you're stalked by a 30-year-old gripping the bulb of a perfume atomizer and, despite her wrinkles, you recognize her as a comer in motion pictures not that long ago. It was creepy, no clouds of My Sin could disguise the stink of failure.

Julia wasn't going to waste a minute crying about anything, she'd do what she had to do, but she just couldn't go *that* route. *Couldn't.* She *had* to succeed. And *would,* if she could concentrate on the one thing only. But the only way to do that was to have a stake to fall back on.

Jack (or whoever he was) said she could count on him, but catering to him alone was already a drag on her progress. Hadn't an assistant director just last week intimated he could help her if only she had evenings free for the exchange of information?

It was possible Jack had served his purpose.

But there was one thing more he could do for her. He could give her that stake.

Smoking, she looked down across the flats towards the Paramount water tower a mile off. The Red Cars ran right past; past RKO and Columbia, too. But MGM required a change, just getting there took an hour and a half. Warner's and Universal were in the Valley — forget about it without a car: two changes, two hours. And here she was, ripening day by day. She had to move the goods in front of the eyes that mattered before they spoiled.

Five years would cost a minimum of $5,000 – *$10,000* to be safe, to have a car; $15,000 and she could buy a little cottage, too, be that much more secure. And security's good for the complexion. Makes a woman radiant. And stars have to radiate their stardom.

If at the end of five years she was not by way of being a star, she'd take a job at Bullock's willingly enough. Oh yes.

So what about Jack? (Whoever.) From Atlanta, he claimed. She could hear traces — traces only. No Southern gentleman, not the way he came home late stinking if a girl let him. Older than she, but had the gall to like women older yet. Mother complex. But mother he never spoke of, father either. Said he was an orphan. Except once said his dad was dead, his mother alive. Another time said the opposite.

Did he come from money? No, no, Dad was born to a Tennessee sharecropper, but went to college, pulled himself up.

And his money? She was secretive herself, but *still*. He wouldn't say a word. He owned the house and Buick outright, and she'd come across two bank books, each showing an opening balance of $10,000 and no withdrawals. She was sure there were more. So he had plenty.

If they got married, it would be a cinch. While it lasted he'd be her security. If it ended, take him for what she could. But Jack swore he'd never marry. (But once he said marry *again*.) By the time she wore him down in that department, she'd be dishing up eggs at Barney's Beanery.

Puffing away, she thought about this John Simons character. Something didn't add up.

A fragment came back to her from a year earlier. They had two days' work together at Metro on a George Raft gangster picture. The scene set in a New York nightclub, they sat at a little round table applauding the floor show, when G-Men raided the place. Melvin Sturgis, in what they called a cameo — the famous, real-life, gangster-buster Melvin Sturgis, just retired from the F.B.I. — led the raid.

It was funny to watch Sturgis in front of the cameras. A star withstands the camera's scrutiny as though it's not there. *She* had that quality. (Had to admit that Jack did, too.) Melvin Sturgis did not. Maybe he was cooler when it was guns and not cameras aimed at him, but for the camera he couldn't walk, couldn't talk, couldn't look anywhere except right into the lens, gaping.

The script called for him to barrel down a staircase and interrupt George Raft's tango with, "Stick 'em up! Federal Bureau of Investigation!"

Sitting in the sun, she snarled, "Stick 'em up! Federal Bureau of Investigation!"

Easy — but not for Melvin.

"Stook 'em up! Oh, damn!" was the first take. The 44th wasn't much better, but at least his legs didn't go spastic and he didn't appeal wide-eyed to the lens while his Tommy gun clattered to the floor. So they took it, overdubbed him for the final release.

She stubbed out her cigarette, drained her coffee cup, sliced a banana over a bowl of Post Toasties. What was it Jack said at some point during the farce? "Melvin Sturgis couldn't catch a flea — much less *me*. And he *tried!*"

Wasn't much to go on, but she had a hunch.

She dressed, put on a hat and dark glasses against the relentless glare that bathes L.A. from spring through fall, pulled on white gloves, walked the block to Sunset and caught a Red Car downtown, to the mosaic-domed Los Angeles Public Library on Bunker Hill.

There she asked if they had newspapers from a year and a half, two years earlier.

They did. They sat her at a refectory table in a lofty room bright with fairy-tale murals, and soon a page rolled up a squeaky-wheeled cart piled with yellowing back copies of the L.A. *Times* and *Herald Examiner*.

She browsed through them. Nothing particularly caught her eye. Lynchings. Grave robberies. Fatal bites from rabid dogs on the loose. More bank robberies than she ever dreamed of, but Jack — *whoever* — wasn't the type.

In issues from September 1934 she read about Bruno Hauptmann's arrest for kidnapping the Lindbergh baby two years earlier. Riveting new details emerged every day. But a month later, a fresh crime swept Hauptmann off the front pages:

# HEIRESS KIDNAPPED!
## *LUCIE SPODE WHITE TAKEN AT GUNPOINT!*

She remembered the case—a national sensation second only to the Lindbergh kidnapping—and at first turned pages impatiently. But three or four days into it, Jack's picture! An out-of-focus snapshot of an engaging kid with younger, thinner features, a different part in his hair and no mustache—and a smile of pure joy—was identified as Harry Thrall, object of a nationwide manhunt. But it was *Jack*, no doubt about it!

The caption plastered beneath it? *"F.B.I. Reward: $10,000."*

*"Aha!"* she said. Couldn't help it. She looked around to see if anyone heard. No one had, save possibly for the silver-haired gent at the next table who, holding her gaze, flicked his lizard tongue across his lips. (An upwards lift of her chin took care of *him!*)

She read on, through front-page accounts of the delivery of a $100,000 ransom, the heiress's release, unharmed, and her kidnapper's disappearance.

For some days, the story lingered on the front pages with sightings of Harry Thrall reported from Portland, Maine to El Paso, Texas to Graz, Austria.

Then it moved to the inside pages, finally vanishing altogether except for occasional Sunday supplement rotogravures of Lucie Spode White in an interesting condition, looking over the gunwales of ocean liners with her husband or coming out of fancy Continental hotels.

Julia thanked the librarians and, in response to their eager query whether she'd found what she was looking for, shrugged with a grateful little moué of disappointment.

Her path lay clear now. Much simplified. *$100,000!* Jack—no, *Harry*—had more than enough to stake her. And if he were disinclined, the F.B.I. reward of $10,000 would suffice. Kismet!

She celebrated with a late lunch at the Biltmore Hotel grille. In a sign of things to come (she hoped!) an RKO film editor pierced her woman-of-mystery persona and, though she rebuffed his first suggestion, gave her his card.

After lunch she walked down through the palms of Pershing Square to Broadway. There she found a pawn shop, made her selection and returned home shortly after 5:00 o'clock.

When Jack—*Harry*—drove up and walked in the door, Julia was sitting on the couch with her pawn-shop purchase in her lap, a little silver-plated .22 pistol.

"Hey, babe."

"Hi, Harry," Julia greeted him, raising the gun.

*"What* did you call me?"

"Marry me, Harry. Gee, that rhymes."

"Not marrying you or anybody else, Julia."

"You'd better, or else give me $50,000, or I'll call the F.B.I."

He lowered himself into a chair, eyes on hers, and put his hands on his knees.

At least he was paying attention.

"Don't be silly, honeybunny. That's all *I* got out of it, was 50,000 bucks."

"Gosh, that's disappointing, when the papers call it a hundred."

"They got it wrong."

"Harry, you're boring me."

"My money's *mine*. After what I went through to get it?"

He looked disgusted and angry—even, for the very first time, a trifle ugly. The shadow of a hawk's wings brushed the window.

"Just giving you a chance to beat the F.B.I. reward, Harry. Sure you won't reconsider?"

He sprang forward. She winged him mid-leap: *Bang!*

Up and down the block dogs started barking.

He fell back into his seat, grabbing his left arm with that ineffable expression of *You shot me!*

"*Shit,* Harry, now it *has* to be the F.B.I., or the cops'll arrest *me.*"

"Go to hell."

She picked up the phone at her elbow and asked the operator to connect her with the F.B.I.

While she waited she said, "I'll admit, you got balls: Parading your face in front of the cameras with nothing but a haircut and mustache between you and a million newspaper photos?"

His good hand smoothing his hair, he said, "Nobody ever sees what's right in front of their face."

# 45.

JOE ALBRIGHT WAS about to go home from his dusty office on Hill Street after another long day grinding away at redemption.

L.A. was thronged with criminals hard at work— *thronged!* — but as the most junior member of the local Bureau, and known to be in the doghouse with the Director — exiled by J. Edgar Hoover after being given the slip by Lucie Spode White's kidnapper — Joe got the stake-outs of Chinese laundries and the interviews with the nuts who claimed to have just seen

Harry Thrall driving down Wilshire Boulevard in a supercharged Cord next to two platinum blondes.

Fine for Melvin Sturgis to come to town, dine at Ciro's, dance at the Cocoanut Grove and do his cameo — Joe snorted at the grapevine's insistence it took him 50 takes to say *"F.B.I."* without a mistake — but Joe was spinning his wheels in L.A.

He was heading for the door, the last one out, when the phone rang. Sighing, he went back and answered it.

"F.B.I., Special Agent Albright speaking."

"Hello, Special Agent Albright," Julia said. "Are you still looking for Harry Thrall?"

"Yeah," Joe answered.

"Keep my name out of it?" No one wants to be called a tattletale.

"Sure."

"And the reward's still good?"

"Ten thousand dollars."

"I just shot him, 2213 Manzanita. Top of the hill above Sunset. My name is Julia Breese."

Her name always came out a whisper.

"Be right there."

Joe made a quick call to Rampart Station. On learning that the police had a report of gunfire at the same address, he requested backup and sped two miles up Sunset in a Bureau Ford, arriving at the same time as an ambulance and four squad cars' worth of shotgun-toting cops.

Drawing his .38 Special, Joe walked up onto a porch latticed with wisteria vines and banged on the door with a forceful *"F.B.I.!"*

"Come in," Julia called.

He went in.

"Hello, Harry. We meet again."

"My name is John Simons, and this bitch *shot* me."

"You're under arrest for the kidnapping of Lucie Spode White."

"Shit."

After a medic fixed a tourniquet to Harry's arm, Joe slipped a handcuff on his wrist like a groom ringing his bride's finger, and led him away.

As the sun sank beyond Santa Monica, Joe's colleagues and the police questioned Julia and searched the house. Up in the hills lightbulbs began to flash, one word at a time, their urgent

**HOLLY**

**WOOD**

**LAND**

The moon slicing the sky with a scimitar's edge, the whole of its wafer palely visible, they took Julia downtown. She knew the moon would be down when she got back, but that the sign would abide.

A good day's work: $10,000, and no more Jack.

## 46.

HARD ON THE HEELS of the kidnapper's capture in Hollywood, tragedy befell the Spode family.

The day after arresting him, Joe Albright and a team of agents flew their prisoner across country, relinquishing him to Falls City's dank, crenellated jail beside the river only after questioning him for more than 24 hours straight.

The next morning, dead tired — if forgivably triumphant — Joe motored out to Indianola Farm. There, in the sunny hedged garden, watching through the balustrades as colts frisked on matchstick legs, he reintroduced himself to Miss Willis, sitting there beside the Old Man, and proposed on the spot. She promptly said yes.

While they cooed and kissed, the Old Man, sitting ignored in his Bath chair, began to thrash. Whether he suffered a seizure, a stroke, a heart attack or simply choked was never ascertained, but whatever it was carried him off instantly. Miss Willis tried to help, Joe ran for the doctor, but Robert Spode, Sr. frothed, lashed out and died, his lips drawn back in a feral rictus.

At 99 years of age he'd outlived every robber baron of his era, save for Rockefeller himself (as ever refusing to come second, Rockefeller clung to life another year).

The Old Man's body was interred in Heaven's Mead in the family's wedding-cake mausoleum, so long ready that moss obscured his name's incised lettering. Every Spode enterprise in Falls City closed down for the funeral, and consequently the city that Friday enjoyed a clean Sabbath sky.

Tragedy continued when Robert Spode Jr.'s wife expired at one of her watering holes. Spode immediately retired from business, vacated Indianola Farm, moved to Naples, Florida, and married his secretary, Miss Bryant.

Miss Willis and Special Agent Albright were married shortly afterwards. If Joe, to his surprise, was denied one hymeneal pleasure, still he was proud of his prize.

## 47.

IN JUNE 1936 HARRY THRALL was put on trial at Falls City's Federal courthouse, in a severe double-cube courtroom. The charges alleged violations of Title 18 of the United States Code Annotated, Sections 408-A, 408-C, 408-O and 1201(a).

Vergil Thrall moved to Falls City for the duration, though his wife stayed home to tend her gardens. He hired for his son the attorney who had won his own case, the one lawyer in Falls City willing to go up against the Spodes.

Ernest Masterson grew up at the Spode Home for the Dismembered, where men whose arms or legs had been torn out by the grinders and conveyors of the Spode cement mills could vegetate decently out of sight; his one-armed father was superintendent. The son grew up with an unaccountable bias against the Spodes, and after joining the bar opposed them at every turn. His successes were not many, of course, but he established a niche for himself.

Harry's trial was a decent, tidy affair that observed the formalities and the unities, and lacked only, given its foreordained result, the element of suspense. It began on Monday, finished on Friday, and dominated the national news all week.

Every seat was taken the first morning, including those in the gallery, but Vergil found a place reserved for him in the row behind the defense table. An oval dome paned with frosted glass served to keep at bay the big heat of a Falls City summer. He took heart from the august mottos painted on the dome's surround.

Soon his son entered, cleanshaven and wearing a blue suit to advantage. U.S. marshals unshackled him (bail of course having been denied) and seated him beside Masterson. Although he turned and smiled reassuringly at his father,

Harry seemed burdened, preoccupation weighing down his old spontaneity.

But his father admired the new gravitas, which he'd noticed also through the glass on his jailhouse visits. The paternal heart discerned tokens of character in the network of lines drawing themselves around mouth and eyes, and in the eyes' expression, slightly vexed, as if seeing farther and deeper than before.

It took all morning to select the jury. Andrews, the prosecutor, liked every prospective juror, but Masterson worked to exclude employees of the Spode enterprises, although he ran out of peremptory challenges short of complete success.

That afternoon Andrews' opening statement assured the jurymen of the government's airtight case against Harry Thrall, whom they had to convict in order to protect their mothers, wives, daughters and other property.

Then it was Masterson's turn.

What Masterson had to say wiped the faces of the jury — judge and spectators, also — with something so rank and disgusting their noses stayed wrinkled the whole week: Not only did he deny the plain fact of kidnapping, he stated that Lucie Spode White *herself* had recruited her *lover* in a harebrained extortion scheme, with the unjust result that she was enriched while her partner in crime was on trial for his life!

The courtroom exploded. After an extended call-and-response of jeers and judicial admonition, decorum was restored, but for the trial's duration, Masterson found it expedient to come and go via the back alley.

TUESDAY MORNING began a three days' parade of prosecution witnesses stitching as tight a case against Harry as eyewitness testimony and forensic science could sew.

Bessie Longworth testified first, with Andrews' help offering a narrative of what she witnessed and identifying Harry as the kidnapper.

But on cross-examination Masterson scored some surprising points.

Bessie agreed that she and Bertram were fired the day after her mistress's release, to languish unemployed for six months, finally on the verge of starving until Pearl White's sister suddenly sought them out and hired them.

Masterson asked if, between those two events, the couple hadn't schemed to blackmail Mrs. White?

Bessie answered so quietly the judge had to ask her to speak up: "I don' remember."

The courtroom stirred uneasily.

But hadn't she and Bertram seen a lawyer and sworn out an affidavit attesting to certain facts connected with the kidnapping?

Bessie couldn't remember.

*Really?* And was it not only days after swearing out that affidavit that White's sister hired them?

She couldn't remember.

Masterson moved to admit the affidavit as an exhibit, but the judge refused after Bessie, handed it by the lawyer and turning it this way and that, failed to recognize it. Instead he was permitted to read from it to try and jog her memory.

When Harry barged into Mrs. White's bedroom, did Bessie not have the impression—as stated in the affidavit—that her mistress knew him? She couldn't remember. Didn't Mrs. White, after bathing, say, "Hurry, let's go"? Couldn't remember. After Mrs. White's return, didn't Bessie find her purse stuffed with cash? No recollection whatsoever.

Masterson placed the affidavit on his table before asking his final question: Didn't she and Bertram, in accepting their new jobs, agree to tear up, destroy, *forget about* their own affidavit?

No recollection, but she did ask Masterson how he got ahold of a copy.

The judge instructed her not to ask questions.

Bessie's testimony made the spectators fan themselves silly, but Vergil's heart bounded: Surely what Bessie couldn't remember already was enough to save his son?

NEXT, LUCIE'S FATHER testified about trying to do Vergil Thrall a good turn by giving his son a job at the Spiral Garage.

Charlie told about firing Harry for borrowing customers' cars, and denied ever seeing him in Mrs. White's company.

Chief Eckerdt spoke of the family's anguish while Mrs. White was gone.

F.B.I. experts testified about finding Harry's fingerprints on the homemade blackjack, the ransom note, in the Indianapolis apartment and Mabel's Chevy, and linked the ransom note to Mabel's Underwood.

Joe Albright told about carrying the ransom to Memphis, and later tracking it, or the cash it was exchanged for, in Harry's possession to Indianapolis. (Harry smiled when he saw Joe, even offered a shy little wave, but Joe set his jaw and ignored him.)

Melvin Sturgis, whose surprise retirement from the Bureau so promptly followed Mrs. White's release, described her shattered condition after her ordeal.

Mabel Thrall voluntarily testified against her ex-husband— she divorced him as soon as she heard about his California liaison—and blamed Harry for everything. She denied that he could have been Mrs. White's lover, or that anybody but he could have conceived or carried out the crime.

What about the pearls and approximately $1,000 she was carrying in a paper bag when arrested?

Harry had nothing to do with them; they were her life savings, which she liked to keep near her (what was unusual about *that?*). And when was she getting them back?

She was bitter, and her testimony damaging.

Day by day, hour by hour, the drumbeat of evidence told, and the jury began to squirm like kids on a road trip: *Were they there yet?*

# 48.

THURSDAY MORNING, the prosecution called its final witness.

"Lucie Spode White!" boomed the clerk, the triple-barreled name rolling through the room. Lucie, in a becoming brown woolen dress with a red-velvet hat, rose from between her father and husband and moved to the witness stand.

In response to Andrews' questions, she described herself as a wife and mother whose principal interests were charitable and who cherished the simple home life she shared with her husband and son.

"Now then, Mrs. White, it pains me that we must speak of certain things," said the prosecutor, glaring at Harry. "I apologize beforehand."

"No need to apologize, Mr. Andrews," Lucie said after the briefest of delays. "I will answer all your questions."

"Do you see in the courtroom the man who bashed your head and dragged you from your home?"

She hardly hesitated. "Yes."

"Will you please point him out to us?"

Lucie pointed to Harry. His father could see his jaw pull in the way it did when he emitted one of his sunny smiles.

"Thank you, Mrs. White. The record will note that the witness indicated the defendant. Did you ever encounter the defendant during his employment at the Spiral Garage?"

She considered and said, "I don't think so. I don't recall it, at any rate. I park my car at the Spiral sometimes, but I'm afraid I don't pay much attention to the attendants."

"You do not recollect meeting the defendant. Do you deny, therefore, having a love affair with him?"

A murmur ran through the courtroom, and the judge banged his gavel. Lucie waited out the fuss, ready with a smile and a very red face.

"I do deny it, with all my heart, Mr. Andrews. I love my husband."

It pained Vergil. The truth would free his son, but surely not him alone? Was Lucie not prolonging her own suffering, her own captivity by lying?

She proceeded to give an account of being snatched from her bed and driven to Indianapolis.

"What happened after you entered that apartment in Indianapolis?"

"He put me in the bedroom closet and locked the door."

"Tell us about that closet."

She faltered. She took a sip of water and a deep breath. Her eyes traveled the room with animal apprehensiveness as she spoke in a voice only just audible.

"It was dark," she said. "I was on the floor. There was nothing in there. Except a bucket. No bedding but a blanket. No water. It was too small to stretch out. The only air came in through a crack at the bottom of the door, and that's all I had. I pushed my nose to that crack and tried to breathe. I thought I would suffocate."

The courtroom was silent, sympathetic, enraptured.

"Thank you," said Andrews, and told Masterson, "Your witness."

Vergil felt sick. He knew the kidnapping was Lucie's idea, and could work out that Harry put her in that closet for the sake ultimately of her own credibility, and thus of their mutual payday, if also in case she changed her mind and tried to leave him holding the bag—as indeed, belatedly, she was doing. But he recognized that her distress was real, and that it meant big trouble for his son.


MASTERSON TOOK A MINUTE to shuffle his notes before rising to his feet to begin cross-examination.

"Good morning, Mrs. White."

"Good morning," Lucie responded crisply a moment later.

"Mrs. White, you identified Harry Thrall as the man who kidnapped you on October 10, 1934, did you not?"

"Yes."

"When did you first meet Harry Thrall?"

"That was our—introduction."

"Really? Earlier that year, didn't he work for several months at one of your family's properties, the Spiral Garage?"

"So I am given to understand."

"But you never met him during that period?"

"If I did, I have no recollection of it."

"Are you surprised to hear that he will tell the jury about having a love affair with you?"

Blood charged her cheeks. "I'm—dismayed. But at this point not surprised."

"An affair first consummated in the Spiral Garage itself? And later at such venues as the Commonwealth Tourist Camp, Welshman's Park, his boarding-house bedroom—"

Andrews drowned him out with objections, while Lucie's

blush lacquered her face pink.

The judge, pointing out that the witness denied meeting Harry Thrall before the kidnapping, told Masterson to move on.

"Mrs. White, with all due respect for you and your undoubted ordeal, wasn't the kidnapping your idea in the first place?"

"Certainly not."

"No? Didn't you suggest to Harry Thrall that he kidnap you—?"

"*No!*"

"—and promise that you would split the ransom?"

"*No!* That is an awful calumny. Certainly not!"

"Didn't you confide to him that you were chronically short of cash—?"

"Never!"

"—but that you had an idea how to improve the situation?"

"Never!"

"A way to collect a portion of your inheritance a few years early?"

"*No!*"

"Mrs. White, let's pretend that you *pretended* to be kidnapped. Are you with me? If you *pretended* to be kidnapped, it couldn't possibly have been a *crime*, could it?"

Her built-in delay permitted the prosecutor to break in with an objection which the judge sustained. He reminded the jury that a very grave crime indeed—a *capital* crime—had been committed and instructed Masterson not to suggest it hadn't.

Masterson took a new tack.

"Mrs. White, your family raised you with a great deal of indulgence, did it not?"

"I don't know what you mean, Mr. Masterson." Lucie dabbed at her eyes. "I do my best to help my city and my community. I'm proud that the name Spode still means something in Falls City."

"You now reside at Indianola Farm, is that correct?"

"Yes."

"Do you receive a housekeeping allowance from your husband, Mrs. White?"

"Yes, like most housewives, I do."

"How large is that allowance?"

"One hundred dollars a week."

"And does $100 a week suffice for your needs?"

"Yes, it does. I was not raised in wealth, whatever you think. We are not wealthy, and this Depression has hit us, too. *Terribly.*"

"Mrs. White, do you really wish it placed on the record that you are not wealthy?"

"I wish it known that I'm expected to run a very sizable house on a small allowance, and that it's not easy."

"Oh? And how many servants do you employ to help you?"

"Objection!" shouted Andrews with another righteous leap to his feet.

The judge sustained it.

Masterson's next question—whether Lucie still insisted that she never knew Harry Thrall before he kidnapped her—brought the prosecutor to his feet again, objecting that it had been asked and answered; Masterson's only prize was the blush painting Lucie's face.

"You've described the harsh conditions of your captivity, Mrs. White," he said. "Did the defendant otherwise comport himself well?"

"Mr. Masterson?"

"Did he molest you?"

"Oh no!" Lucie said, recoiling. "I told him if he did

anything of *that* sort my husband would never stop until he'd killed him."

"In other words, the defendant behaved like a gentleman?"

"Oh, yes." She snapped open her pocketbook and brought out a handkerchief, adding, as she dabbed at her eyes, *"Throughout."*

"No more questions, Your Honor."

The witness, excused, stepped impassively from the stand to take her seat again between husband and father. That evening, in describing the war of wits between victim and lawyer, the Falls City *Truth* handed Lucie victory's laurel.

## 49.

THE GOVERNMENT rested its case. Only the last formal element of a trial—the defense, acknowledged as necessary even to a foregone conclusion—remained to be played out.

It took but Thursday afternoon and Friday morning.

First, calling to the stand the proprietor of the Commonwealth Tourist Camp, Masterson grilled him about Harry's and Lucie's assignations. But the proprietor not only denied ever having seen either of them, he declared his camp hadn't even been in existence until *after* the kidnapping. Further, indignantly, he protested that, as a Christian, he never extended its comforts to unmarried fornicators.

When Masterson produced a register showing the preponderance of the name *Smith* among his guests, the proprietor noted that it's a common name.

Masterson's frustration deepened when he called Mrs.

Brown, Harry's cookie-baking fellow boarder, to the stand. Mrs. Brown, supremely nervous, and for reasons known only to herself wearing a heavy veil behind which her eyes flitted like birds, although acknowledging that she recognized Harry, denied ever entertaining him in her room, much less baking him Toll House cookies. Instead she stated that his well-known freshness towards the gentler sex had caused her always to keep a safe distance from him.

Then their landlady Mrs. Good denied ever finding Harry in a female boarder's room, and resented the insinuation.

Masterson called his next witness, Donovan A. Jester, IV. This occasioned a delay as the jury was sent out and Jester, a burly figure in prison stripes, shackled at wrists and ankles, was escorted into the courtroom. He was an inmate of the State penitentiary. After much fussing with keys, much clanking of iron, he was unshackled, seated in the witness box and the jury brought back in.

Jester was 27, sandy-haired, his face blocky but good-looking. In a suit he would have resembled his father, the dapper President of the Falls City Trust sitting in the last row. But the taint of prison adhered to the son. Pallid and fleshy, he had a bad haircut and furtive manner. When he scratched his nose or turned his neck, stick-figure tattoos of his own cellblock handiwork peeped into view at wrist and collar.

Masterson, reminding him of their prior conversation in prison, asked if he knew Lucie Spode White.

"Know Lucie?" Jester responded, his features softening. "We were playmates. Known each other since before I can remember. Our fathers are friends, too. But after she married naturally we saw less of each other."

"Mr. Jester, why are you in prison?"

"I held up a Super-Six gas station. With a gun."

"And why ever would a promising lad like you do such a

thing?"

"Guess I needed money, or thought I did."

"Whose idea was it?"

"The devil's, I believe, sir, or whatever it is they put in moonshine. 'Cause one day I was drunk on hooch and wanted more, but had no money, so I robbed the Super-Six."

"All right, I'm sure we must give the devil his due. But here in our mundane terrestrial world, whose idea was it to rob the Super-Six?"

"Mine, sir."

Masterson looked perplexed.

"When I spoke to you at State prison, didn't you tell me that *Mrs. White* suggested you rob it? That it was *her* idea? To finance a weekend away together?"

Amidst a general intake of breath, of disgust at this return of Masterson's *idée fixe*, all eyes swiveled to Lucie. Blushing very bright, she held her head upright, features rigid.

"No, sir," Jester said. "You misunderstood me. That was my plan all the way."

Lucie's chin lifted in approval.

"What did you get?"

"Five years, another three when I tried to escape."

"I mean from the robbery?"

"Thirty-five dollars, something like that. But they caught me three days later."

"Were you alone when you robbed the station?"

"Did it myself, yes, sir."

"But didn't witnesses place somebody in your car?"

"Sir?"

"At your trial two witnesses testified they saw somebody, never identified, waiting in your car while you were inside robbing the attendant, did they not?"

"Why, I'm ashamed to admit it, but at the Bandits Club that

evening Pearl White asked me to drive his wife home, and it was on the way there that I stopped to rob the Super-Six. It was an impulse. *She* had no idea what I was doing."

Jester glanced again at Lucie. Her husband lifting her to her feet, the next moment she was leaving the courtroom within his embrace. All eyes followed.

Masterson took five thoughtful steps in one direction, five in the other, awaiting the return of all eyes.

"Mr. Jester, you left the Bandits Club drunk on *hooch?*"

"Prohibition was still on," offered Jester.

"And you admit Lucie Spode White was actually waiting in your car while you robbed the gas station?"

"Yes, sir."

"Mr. Jester, are you *sure* she didn't suggest the robbery to you?"

"Oh, no, sir, she knew nothing. Just told her hold tight a minute while I used the Chick Sales. It was that devil hooch, like I said before."

He averred this with a pride admired by almost everybody who heard him.

"I see. But didn't you use the proceeds of the robbery to take Mrs. White to a tourist camp for the weekend?"

There was a general jeer at the audacity of the question.

"No, *sir!*" Jester said loudly, clearly shocked.

"Where were you arrested, three days after the robbery? At a library? In church?"

Jester stirred uncomfortably. "Well, at a tourist camp near Fontainebleau, but —"

"Was Mrs. White with you?"

"No, *sir!*"

"Mr. Jester, if you had the chance to do things over, would you rob that gas station?"

Jester opened his mouth, but closed it again. The courtroom

suddenly went dead silent. Watching the young man was as distasteful as eating barbecue while pigs scream in the slaughterhouse next door. But sacrifices must be made.

"No, sir," Jester said quietly, "don't know that I would."

"Your witness," said Masterson, but Andrews had no questions.

The light in Jester's eyes died. The jury was sent out, he submitted to his irons and laboriously dragged himself out of the courtroom, while the judge warned Masterson that his remaining witnesses had better testify about the crime they were there to try.

## 50.

FIRST THING FRIDAY MORNING, the clerk called out Harry Thrall's name.

Harry stood up and walked to the witness chair.

Masterson wished the jury to see a well-spoken, educated, guileless young man, and it did. Harry was frank and open, and everything he said was true. With the retrospective pride and pleasure of a young man to whom that sort of thing tended to happen, he recounted meeting Lucie and starting an affair with her.

His father's heart broke watching him testify with minutely accurate workings of lips and teeth, punctilious with dates and times and places, eyes earnest and brow crinkled—adorable as a little boy determined to get it right.

"How old are you, Harry?"

"I'm 26 now."

"Do the ladies like you?"

"Don't know about *that*, sir." Dimples. "I like *them* fine."

There was nervous laughter.

"Was Mrs. White one of the ladies you liked?"

"Yes, sir."

"You knew she was married, didn't you?"

"Yes, I did."

"Then why pursue an affair with her?"

"Figured that was her business. And I could tell she liked her fun."

Harry told of talking car-to-car with Lucie driving down Falls Road, and later seeing her ride the manlift at the Spiral Garage, and was beginning to tell about putting the Auburn's seat flat, when the judge firmly stopped him and instructed the jury to disregard.

His accounts of their other assignations were similarly suppressed, especially the one at Welshman's Park where she first suggested he kidnap her.

"And on October 10, 1934, *did* you kidnap Lucie Spode White?"

"No, *sir*. I did enter her home on a subterfuge, I admit it — went right into her bedroom, pretending to be a telephone repairman. And I did drive her up to Indianapolis that day, but she came willingly. You can't call it kidnapping. She suggested that I do it. Her idea from the start."

"But you hit her on the head and put her in a closet and locked her in, is that correct?"

"Yes, sir."

"Why would you be so cruel?"

"If the cops or F.B.I. came in, it had to look real. The only way for it to *look* real was for it to *be* real."

"You collected a ransom. Did you intend to share that ransom with her?"

"Yes, sir, going halfsies was the idea—*her* idea—from the start."

"But getting that ransom from the Spode family amounted to extortion, didn't it?"

"Maybe so, though it was *her* money that she just wanted to get a little early. If you insist, I guess I knew I was helping her with extortion."

"In the event, *did* you share the ransom with her?"

"Yes, sir."

"Despite being on the run and chased by the F.B.I.?"

"Yes, sir."

"How did you get her half—her $50,000—to her?"

"Drove through the night from Wickliffe Mounds in Kentucky, where my father gave it to me, to Indianapolis, with a G-Man on my tail."

"Surely it was perilous—even *silly*—to postpone your escape until you'd first returned to Indianapolis?"

"But I had to do it, you see."

"You heard Mrs. White deny that you brought her that money?"

"I did."

"And your former wife denies it, too?"

"Yes. But I know what I did. I gave Lucie—Mrs. White—her half of the ransom."

"And what, today, is your opinion of Lucie Spode White?"

He looked at her. She looked away.

"A fine lady, a real thoroughbred. But I'm disappointed she won't own up to things."

For whatever reason, Andrews had no questions for Harry.

As his son left the stand, Vergil was satisfied that in some measure the truth had been heard.

Not that it mattered.

THE LAWYERS MADE their closing arguments before lunch.

Painting Harry in horrific colors, Andrews registered outrage at the defense's attempt to smear the victim.

Masterson painstakingly went over the whole chain of evidence and expressed confidence the jury would agree that sufficient doubt had been cast on it to oblige them to free his client.

After lunch the judge read his instructions to the jurymen, and they gravely filed out to begin their deliberations.

An hour later they had a verdict.

In his heart Vergil had always known they would feel compelled to punish Harry for society's own hypocrisy, yet as they entered the room he scanned their faces hopefully.

But he saw his son's fate in their eyes, and slumped as the foreman delivered the inevitable conclusion and asked the judge if the jurymen could get rides home. His Honor was pleased to order it, further instructing the deputies to sound their sirens if so requested. He then dismissed them and, without pausing, sentenced Harry to be electrocuted in Atlanta on July 7.

It meant a great deal to Vergil that the first thing Harry did after taking in the news was to turn around and smile at him.

# 51.

AFTER BRIEFLY RETURNING home to comfort his wife, Vergil went to Atlanta.

Meanwhile Masterson appealed the verdict. He warned

father and son that the appeal would fail, and he was right: Though the trial efficiently excluded the truth of the case, it was procedurally correct and Harry — especially as the first person convicted under the Lindbergh Law — had to burn.

Vergil presented himself at Atlanta Federal Prison the day after Harry arrived there, and was pleased and touched when the warden offered him daily visits in his son's cell if he consented to undergo a search every time.

"Thank you, yes, that's fine," said Vergil. They searched him, and he followed a guard to the Death House.

The Death House, a structure ancient in 1936 — a squat stone building with a castellated roofline — was set in one corner of an immense dirt yard. It housed inmates condemned to death. Near it against the prison wall stood an old unpainted barn with a sheet-metal smokestack. The barn once held the gallows and now housed the electric chair.

Vergil's knees wobbled as he approached the Death House, but he made it inside. His eyes had to adjust to the gloom, and his nose to the smell.

The guard stopped at one riveted iron door among others and unlocked it.

Vergil peered inside. A square of reflected light wavered on the rear wall.

"Harry? *Harry!*"

"Dad."

They wrapped their arms around each other, touching for the first time since Vergil delivered the ransom nearly two years earlier. Each felt changes. The elder had lost his office softness, and Harry, still slender, had something newly resistant about him, too.

They sat on the bunk and talked, at first haltingly, but soon with fluency. The father was astonished and pleased by the alteration in his son. The callow youth geared for pleasure had become a different man—a man indeed, accepting everything, blaming nobody; plenty regretful, to be sure, but acknowledging that what happened to him was ultimately his own fault.

Neither referred to the event looming in July. Vergil wanted to assure Harry of what two different electrical linemen assured him, that the shock of great voltage is a painless blow; more an invasive preoccupation rather distantly perceived until unconsciousness arrives via the inability to breathe.

For his part, Harry spared his father Death House scuttlebutt about clothes burning off and heads exploding in flame. Nor did he point out the corner of the yard where his charred body would be dropped in the ground, its location plotted on graph paper locked away in an office.

Weeks passed, and the Fourth of July, a Saturday, made Atlanta blaze and boom late into the night.

Monday morning—morning of the fatal day—Vergil went early to the prison. He was to be allowed to witness the event if he wished. Though he had no heart for it, he would let Harry choose whether he wanted him there. They had until a minute after midnight.

They sat on Harry's bunk sharing memories of those old road trips to St. Louis, highlights of Harry's childhood: Up the great river and crossing by ferry that they might stop at the Wickliffe Mounds, vying to be the first to crow, *"I spy!"*

The father took the son's hand in his.

They were talking of what grand repast Harry might order for dinner, when the Warden entered the cell with a smile that at first struck Vergil as tasteless in the extreme.

"News, gentlemen: President Roosevelt has commuted the sentence to life imprisonment. Prisoner, prepare for transfer to Cellblock D."

## 52.

HARRY THRALL WAS soon moved to Alcatraz, as befitted his status as one of the most notorious criminals in captivity. His father also moved to San Francisco.

Vergil visited whenever allowed — which was not often; the rules of Alcatraz were strict. He would press his hand to his son's on the wire grille so hard that after a visit its heel looked char-broiled.

Their conversation, however banal, was essential to both. Vergil offered little vignettes of daily life as a retired gentleman in a new clime. Harry gave cheerful accounts of his fellow inmates and his reading and the weather, even if he experienced the weather only in a narrow stone yard that resembled the bottom of a well. He always said goodbye with, "Be good, Pops!"

Vergil died of a heart attack one day at the Public Library.

A few years later, pasty and bald, but with his dimples holding good, Harry, deemed less a threat, was transferred to Leavenworth Prison, and assigned to help tend its fields of vegetables and flowers. Growing lean and nut-brown in the Kansas sun, he took to it, especially to cultivating flowers, which then were sold locally. Flowers came to fill his days, days filled with work and incident, suspense and satisfaction; his dreams, too. His peonies earned regional fame.

Even years later, when he was getting old and it cost him groans to get in the dirt, he dug and planted, pruned and weeded with joy — partly from thinking about the people his flowers would gladden.

Younger cons, intent on doing the least work they could contrive to do, jeered at him as they leaned on their spades, but Harry declared there was *freedom* in the dirt, that sweating in the sun and growing things made up a large part of *his* life's goodness, and that he loved his life.

To the derision *this* fetched, he responded that he, like they, belonged where he was.

"We got caught," he said. "That's what those of us inside have in common: *Us* they caught. Others they haven't yet, maybe never will, but *us* they did. And we're guilty, be sure of that. Never met an innocent man yet. They'll tell you I'm doing time for kidnapping? Really it's for *rape*. So we're where we're supposed to be, and we might as well make the best of it."

He named his flower garden *Paradise*.

Harry Thrall died in 1981 after a short illness, shackled to a bed in the prison infirmary, but with his face turned to the sunshine streaming in. He was buried in good Kansas earth.

JULIA BREESE GOT her stake in the form of the F.B.I. reward, and doubled it selling a newspaper serial about life with the *Spode Kidnap Monster* — the fee easing the annoyance of being called a tattletale — but never became a movie star.

She did, however, marry a cameraman, and though that marriage didn't work out, she discovered a talent for marrying up. Five weddings, four divorces and a distinguished widowhood netted her a home in Bel-Air, a beach house near Point Dume, a cottage in Montecito, a strip mall on Normandie Avenue and an ample stock portfolio to go along with her weirdly unchanging appearance.

MABEL THRALL dropped out of sight; her fate is not known.

MELVIN STURGIS fatally shot himself in the head one day in 1960 while cleaning his pistol.

HIS CAPTURE OF Harry Thrall put Joe Albright on the star track at the F.B.I., and he put in a long and useful career there, investigating leftists, wiretapping civil-rights leaders, harassing John Lennon. He and his wife, living in perfect concord, raised a large family and lived to ripe old ages.

BESSIE LONGWORTH, widowed early, became a housekeeper in the Spode Tower, emptying wastebaskets and dusting offices there into her 80s.

PEARL WHITE prospered at Indianola. Acquiring more fire engines, he kept them in high polish, and also built a two-mile, quarter-scale steam railroad with complicated crossings and a fleet mixed of passenger and freight cars, with locomotives whose piercing whistles had him continually being hauled into court by the neighbors. He discreetly enjoyed his mistresses elsewhere; if no longer faithful to his wife, he remained loyal.

Pearl delighted in Robert Spode White, whose strangely distant mother left the daily tasks of childrearing to a team of European professionals. Lucie didn't seem to know what to do with the boy, alternately loving him and resenting him, wanting to smother him or exile him to Siberia.

Bobby somehow took it all in stride, a young force of nature, a cheerful and popular soul, dark and good-looking (the family at a loss to find an ancestor he resembled), with an infectious smile—rich by any estimation, and merry about it.

If he didn't inherit his great-grandfather's single-minded devotion to growing his fortune, after all there was no need; the money multiplied seemingly by itself. It furnished him with his houses and boats and planes, his women and his collection of Bentleys, and also, late in life, assisted his devotion to the Nature Conservancy and Rainforest Foundation.

LUCIE SPODE WHITE, as her son's mother, her husband's wife, her father's daughter, the Old Man's granddaughter, and a member of a community peculiarly webbed with calcified ancient connections, was burdened with social expectations and obligations. She met them all, always — never shirked.

But she refused to talk about her kidnapping. Quite naturally, especially at first, people were curious about it and sometimes, with no intention of being rude, ventured to ask about it. But any such question instantly coated her with shellac; she cut off eye contact and, if necessary, performed a sweeping pirouette that left her questioner tottering and exposed.

Over time, fewer questions were posed.

She found two great interests as she endured her long life.

By some law of irony, Lucie, like Harry Thrall, took solace in flowers, especially in roses. Transforming the hedged garden at Indianola Farm into a rose garden, she made it famous. When visitors came she retreated to the house, but watched as they passed among her rosebushes, taking vicarious pleasure in their enjoyment.

She spent endless hours cultivating varieties new and old, perfecting the form of the bud, the color of the blossom. To rest amidst her labors, she'd sit on a bench and watch foals and mares cavort; rest, then dig and clip and manure some more.

The other passion was movies. She built a screening room and added a projectionist to her household staff. For decades she watched ten or 12 films a week. Cary Grant and Humphrey Bogart were her favorite stars, but she also ran over and over again the movies Harry Thrall proudly mentioned at trial as those in which he figured as a background extra, and watched hundreds of others, too, from the period of his Hollywood sojourn.

Most were forgettable, and not improved by her focus on the mute figures passing behind the action or sitting in the shadows. Many of them told the then-popular tales of high-society millionaires, representing a world she'd actually known but which, as time went on, receded tantalizingly out of reach.

And occasionally from among the figures flickering in black and silver, one would jump out at her so forcibly she felt the reality of her life (such as it was) waver — felt her vitality leach onto the screen. He never spoke a word, never caught an eye, never sought to upstage so much as a potted plant, but, ever young and glossy, as directed sat or walked (with a snap to the wrists) or pretended to talk, merely occupying a patch of the screen; and yet that patch was meaningful to her.

CPSIA information can be obtained
at www.ICGtesting.com
Printed in the USA
BVHW031145010421
603934BV00007B/53

9 781736 833308